WORLDS ON FIRE

A Short Story Collection

RAYMOND S FLEX

CONTENTS

THE PORT-AU-PRINCE PARADOX

I N THE DISTANCE, Marie Gedeon could still hear the *rumble* of falling objects.

The screams cutting through the air in the street outside.

Closer to where she remained prone, in a catlike position, on her hands and knees—hunched beneath the wooden table her father claimed to have cobbled together from washed-up wood he'd hand gathered from the baie de Port-au-Prince, the gateway to Haiti—she could hear the percussive strikes as lumps of plaster and hunks of timber dropped from the ceiling and onto the upper floorboards of her own home:

The home which'd been in her family for four generations.

Almost a hundred years now.

The home which her great-grandfather had often bragged about building with his own two hands, although Marie had her own theory that neighbours; or contractors, architects, might've —*perhaps*—lent a helping hand . . .

It was somewhat hard to believe that the elegant support timbers made of greenheart wood—the neatly carved plaster cornices on the skirting boards about the house and on the staircase banisters, the neat, smooth marble fountain in the courtyard— had all been her grandfather's direct responsibility. And all this when her great-grandfather, like all the men in her family, had been a lawyer. Still, she supposed, being a grandmother herself now, that she better understood *why* her great-grandfather might've told one, or more, tall tale in his life. Sometimes fiction was better than truth. More *interesting*, at the very least.

She waited patiently for the sounds of tumbling to stop, so that she might scramble out from beneath the table, try to lose the hard pain in her bare kneecaps and at the heels of her hands from being in this crouched position for so long. Already she was doubtful that she would be able to get to her feet without stumbling, or even falling, several times. It wasn't only the impact of what surrounded her —the *shock* of what had just happened, was *still* happening—but she had had, for many years now, stiff joints. She would often joke about it to neighbours, about how whenever she got up from a chair it was akin to her attempting to start her old sixties-era Ford 500.

That it'd take her at least three tries.

The sound of rumbling continued.

From above.

From outside.

People called out.

Called for help.

She could taste blood. When she reached up to her mouth, her finger came away with a thin, brownish-red smear. She swallowed away the dryness in her throat, and turned her attention back to her kitchen. She looked over to the stove.

The large steel pot of rice continued to bubble away. She had been tending to it when she first felt the ground giving way beneath her feet. It was a little akilter now, but remained standing on its metal support. The stove wasn't hooked up to the mains gas, or electricity. It had its own gas canister stowed neatly below which, faithfully, continued to supply the neat, bright-blue, glowing ring of flame beneath the pot. Already, from years and years of experience, she could sense the giveaway burning odour; the odour of the rice sticking to the bottom of the pot. That smell which always, no matter where she was in the house, or what she was doing, made her want to rush out and go tend to the kitchen. Right now, it didn't matter how ridiculous she might look to any passer-by in her Bermuda shorts and sky-blue plastic Crocs sandals—the only footwear she ever felt anything *near* comfortable these days, what with her swollen feet.

If only her ancestors could see how she dressed herself now!

She left the stove to its own whims, staying put beneath the table.

It was just as well because, only a second or so after the thought had departed her brain, a large chunk of plaster came free from the ceiling and—with a gut-churning *creak*—fell.

It smashed onto the black-and-white kitchen tiles.

Fragments scattered all over.

Dust puffed up.

She reached out and dragged the neck of the baggy, beige t-shirt she wore to bed up and over her nostrils and mouth, to guard against the dust. She had to turn her face away so that she wouldn't swallow the worst of it. She could feel her heart fluttering against her ribs, and the flush of heat in her cheeks. A year or so ago, she had had her first heart attack. She hoped another wasn't on its way. But if now was her time, then she supposed there was nothing she could do.

She had had three children, and those three children had each had children of their own.

Seven grandchildren in all.

The clan would continue.

She felt a shifting weight in the pocket of her Bermuda shorts. Acting on instinct, she reached out, took hold of the solid, lumpy mass. A pocket watch—*the* pocket watch which she kept with her at all times:

Sturdy, scratched-up silver casing.

Roman numerals.

The bow and crown kept well-oiled.

It was a sort of lucky charm. It had been passed down the generations, from male to male, until Marie—being the only child of her parents—had at last claimed it.

She kept the pocket watch with her at all times except when she took her morning shower—when she would leave it on the soft walnut surface of her bedside table. If she decided to draw herself an evening bath, she would prop the watch up on the rim and stare at those slender, simple hands.

Time passing by.

The ever-vanishing hours, minutes—*seconds*.

Surely the times when her well-intentioned children had chided her for taking the pocket watch out of the house—afraid it may be lost, stolen or broken—numbered in the thousands, if not *tens* of thousands. But she knew she needed to keep it close.

Always.

As she tuned herself back into the world—the still-falling rubble—she realised that she could hear a child's wail.

Coming from upstairs.

Sébastien.

At six years old, he was her youngest grandchild.

She had been looking after him for the past week, while his parents were vacationing in Cancún, Mexico.

"*Granmè!*"

He spoke the creole word inured with his North American father's language.

Although it was difficult to ignore him—*far* more difficult, of course than ignoring the rice sticking to the bottom of the pan—she knew that there was no option.

She turned the pocket watch over.

Rumour had it that the pocket watch was over two hundred years old, and from the times of Henri Christophe, the first king of Haiti. That it had been brought across the Atlantic by some French colonist who had, perhaps, been relieved of the pocket watch in the War of Independence. The waves etched onto the silver casing had always supported the theory that this *was* indeed from a French colonist, given to him as a token of appreciation.

6

But, again, like everything else in Marie's family history, it was a matter of debate. All she knew for a fact was the inscription on the casing, half obscured by an aged, brown stain—blood?

She examined it now, as she had done a million times before:

Pour Mon Amour

So read the florid inscription from this theoretical Frenchman's wife, or lover.

She shifted her gaze downward, to the only other writing on the case, and which Marie had once always believed to be the maker's name, or, perhaps, some sort of an inside joke between the giver and the receiver of the pocket watch:

Ministère de Cieux Bleus

The Ministry of Blue Skies.

Outside, the sounds of falling debris seemed to have stopped. They had slowed in their frequency at the very least. She turned the pocket watch over in her palm, saw that the hands had ceased to turn—at precisely five p.m.

Yes, it was time.

She reached up, turned the crown a dozen or more times, just as her father—the one who had presented her the watch—had shown her.

Feeling the odd, familiar humming sensation in her chest, she felt herself gliding away. That brief moment of absolute power, before an aeroplane takes off. Its engines all firing as hard as possible.

Just an inch away from achieving flight.

When she opened her eyes, turned, she saw that she was wearing the leaf-green cocktail dress, a pair of sleek, high heels which matched. The smell of perfume clung to her. It smelled lightly of peaches. Her dark skin was smooth—*sleek*—how it had been before years of motherhood had done with her. Although the same process passed over her each time she shifted away from the real world, and into the fantastical—that which *surely* never was except in her own mind—she was surprised at her appearance:

Young.

That same twenty-eight she had been when her father, gasping his last as he succumbed to throat cancer in a private ward of Hôpital de la Trinité, had passed her the pocket watch, explained its intricacies. She hadn't had time to ask questions of him, to confirm that what he had told her, the muttered words about the watch's properties to jump through time and space, into other worlds, were the ramblings of a dying man. She had had time to discover that for herself.

She took in her surroundings, the long, narrow corridor, much more slender than she might have brought to mind if somebody had asked her to describe the End of Time:

The Ministry of Blue Skies

The floors were of sleek, black marble; the wallpaper of black velvet.

Every six or seven paces, there were old-style, burning torches hanging down from the walls. Their light was unlike normal flames. For one, the light didn't carry as far as normal, real-world flames. It was silver and crept upward from the base of each torch, shedding a sort of semi-obscure moonlight glow about the corridors.

There were always shadows.

Up ahead.

Behind.

To her left.

To her right.

As she passed by the doors—all of them that same smooth, greenheart wood that was used for the timbers in her home—she read off the bronze plaques on each door. Strange markings were engraved on each of the plaques, in a bright, white ink, or paint, whatever it was the first to come here had used. The markings were from a strange language which she—without explanation, and without any effort to learn—spoke fluently.

They all indicated dates.

And although there was no sequential order which she could observe, she already knew, on instinct, where any given time or place might be.

As she walked along the corridor, she heard the dim echo of her heels clacking behind her. There was no near-distance echo at all. The sound came exclusively from a long way behind—a long way *down*, it seemed—as if she was listening to the skittering of rocks at the bottom of a well.

Whenever she was back in her home, in the real world, she often wondered to herself just how she managed to concentrate when she came here.

To have an *eternity* all spread out before her.

The entire *history* of her island, all here, and waiting.

Yet it was single-minded focus, she told herself, which allowed her to ever return from this place.

She looked over the doors as she passed by, her eyes hardly seeing, all those runes and etchings on the plaques snagging onto some part of her brain. She allowed them to blow against her, like the tropical breeze of baie de Port-au-Prince. And tonight—because here, at the End of Time it was *always* night—she knew exactly where she was headed. Just what she needed to do, if she was to save her grandchild. She had to go and see the Administrators.

It was only when she came to a certain door—not the door to the Administrators—that she ceased her advance along the corridor. She stood and stared at the plaque, her mind sifting over the runes: a strange rounded squiggle—almost like a coiled-up spring. Something deep within her explained clearly what the squiggle meant. Something which could only have been passed through her blood, like a gift . . . or a curse.

A genetic *disorder* . . .

The year behind the door was 1962.

A world long ago past, like all the other worlds which awaited behind each door.

And because time stood still here—and because she knew, with a quiet confidence, that she might never get this chance again—she reached out for the brass doorknob.

Turned.

When she opened her eyes, she found herself standing on Avenue de la République in downtown Port-au-Prince. It was night-time. The air was thick, full of moisture. She could taste the salt of the sea, entering through her airways, being breathed deep to the pits of her lungs. Of course, she wore the same cocktail dress from before.

Nobody was around.

All was quiet.

Deathly quiet.

She could see the bright, white pillars of the Palais National all lit up with bright orange lights.

There was no other light source.

Not even the moon above.

Those blinking, shimmering lights of the slums on the hillsides no longer shone either.

No streetlights.

She looked to the Palais National, and to the wrought-iron gates surrounding. They seemed to have been painted recently. As she approached the palace fence, she was surprised that there was no pain. None of the usual pain which accompanied walking; her comfortable Crocs, or not.

She peered in through the railings, only realising that she still held the watch when she reached up to clasp hold of the cool iron.

Not having anywhere to keep the watch, she instead allowed the hand clasping it to fall down to her side, and used her other—*free*—hand to take hold of the railing.

She had been to the palace before, of course.

In fact, her grandfather had been good friends with a succession of presidents.

But it was very different to show up at the palace wearing . . . well, something like what she wore right now . . . and to see the cars filing their way around the driveway, all of them finely polished, and some with pearly streamers running their way from the bonnet to the windows, flapping in the air wafting in from the Caribbean. She recalled, very clearly, returning from those dinners.

The very first time she visited the palace she must've been thirteen, or fourteen. They had driven out through the palace gates and passed by a group of children—*her own age*—in nothing but rags, emaciated frames, holding their dirtied palms open to them, praying for some offering.

She clearly recalled that her mother would lightly shield her eyes with her gloved hand, as if her eyes had been struck by the unbearable glare of a photographer's bulb.

Marie had never forgotten those children; or the circumstances of the place where she lived. But, as the years went by, the family fortunes declined. This was mainly due to her father's reluctance for Marie to go into the family business, holding out, seemingly, for a son.

Marie realised that the means her family might've possessed to make a difference to those children—and many others—had diminished.

As she stood in her younger body, she thought about how she had had so many grand plans, and how not a one had come to fruition. And how the house she lived in now—and would till her dying days—represented the very last of her family's legacy.

The house and the Ford 500.

With a slight sigh, she turned away from the palace.

She had wanted to come here.

Just one final time.

Before she left for good.

She turned her attention back to the pocket watch, and she turned it on another few notches.

Back in the slender corridor at the End of Time, Marie squinted, becoming once more accustomed to the ethereal, silver light from the torches. She breathed in deeply, still catching the vague scent of the salty breeze, and that slightly fruity, tropical flavour at the back of her throat.

The worlds were *always* like that.

Stagnant.

Unmoving.

Lit as if by memory.

But she was glad they existed.

Before she had more time to speculate on what she had seen —on those thoughts which'd rattled through her head like popcorn kernels near explosion—she continued down the corridor, her eyes fixed on the gloom opening out ahead. She felt the silvery glow of the torches brush against her skin, *caressing* her almost. She didn't stop at any other doors before she reached the one she knew, in her gut, belonged to the Administrators.

She paused for a long few moments, knocked twice, and then turned the doorknob.

The air within smelled strongly of cinnamon, as it always did, almost like somebody might've been burning a joss stick. It almost knocked her backward.

All around, she saw the workings of the Ministry of Blue Skies.

The large, ceiling-to-floor windows, beyond which there was nothing save a bright, white light. A light which she couldn't stand looking at directly. She had to bring her forearm up to shield her eyes from the glare. Or else turn her gaze away.

People sat at their desks.

Tapping away at electric typewriters.

Others with phones crooked between shoulder and ear.

All of them dressed smartly in their suits and ties, and skirts and blouses.

Seventies fashions.

Marie had always thanked her lucky stars to have been born into family money—to never have had to run the gauntlet through one of these cubicle farms: these *offices*. That the very worse which she had found herself facing was the odd lecherous 'acquaintance' of her father, clearly seeing her as trophy-wife material or else as an obedient—*naïve*—little fling.

But she had always been able to defend herself.

And, when it had become too much, she had taken her father's old service pistol, kept it in her purse. After that she hadn't had any further problems.

She eyed the office workers, all of them one-hundred-percent focussed on the task at hand, whatever that task was.

Nobody stopped her as she approached the door, this time marked in official French:

Administrateurs

There was no reason to knock.

They already knew she was coming.

She simply pushed open the door.

Often, back in the real world, she wondered why the Administrators appeared to her in her own language, and in the dress of her own time. She wondered what her father might've seen when he had come here, to the End of Time—to the Ministry of Blue Skies.

And then she wondered what her grandfather might've seen.

And all those before him.

The trio of Administrators sat behind their desk: one man, and two women; all of them sat with their hands clenched together, all watching Marie walk in through the doorway, with a sort of catlike fascination. They all wore neat and tidy suits, all of them of the same black marble shade as the corridor outside. The man with a crisp white shirt underneath—a perfectly knotted, black tie—and the women with white blouses, undone a couple of buttons to show off their supple, thirty-something throats.

The walls of the room were glass. Bright white light flooded in through them.

She addressed the Administrators. "Dearest *Mesdames et Messieurs*, I have come here to ask for a favour."

There was no movement in any of their faces.

Not so much as the stirring of an eyebrow.

The twitch of a lip.

She awaited some sort of acknowledgement, knowing that it would be presumptuous—let alone *rude*—for her to proceed into what she wanted without their blessing. Her eyes skittered between the assembled trio, finally coming to rest on the woman who sat in the middle, and who gave her a sombre, definite nod.

Marie drew a deep breath.

Then told her what she needed.

Marie felt the floorboards creaking beneath the soles of her Crocs as she crept toward the spare room—the room which had once been her own nursery, and where her grandson, Sébastien, was staying now.

Her aches and pains were back.

The *heaviness* of her strides.

She thought to her daughter's apprehension, how she had insisted, almost to the point of tears, that Marie travel to Miami, stay in their apartment while she looked after Sébastien.

But Marie had had no intention of that.

Many years ago, she had made a promise to herself that, no matter what happened, she would never again leave the island. It would mean her death.

What her daughter had never understood was that, here, in her house, Sébastien was far safer than he ever might be in that apartment of theirs.

With Marie here to protect him.

She stepped in through the doorway to Sébastien's bedroom, still feeling the slight tremors passing through the floorboards, the creaking of the timbers threatening to give way at any second. She caught the whiff of those baby smells, that clean scent of soap. She knew, in a few years, Sébastien would lose those pleasant odours, that he would grow up to be an adult, just as happened with the rest of mankind. She looked down at him, lying on his side, in the slender single bed, his blankets all bundled up over him, as if he might be able to make the whole world disappear by simply draping them over his head.

She remembered when she'd thought shew might have the power to make the world disappear.

Those had been much happier days.

She sat down on the edge of the mattress, feeling a slight tremble passing over her. In her right hand she continued to clench the pocket watch tight. She could feel its silver casing made warm by her hold. Already, outside, she could hear the never-ending sound of sirens.

The cries of grief—the shouts for help.

She looked down at Sébastien, his father's clear, blue eyes drawn wide more with curiosity than fear. She knew that it was her calmness which relaxed him, which stopped him from feeling frightened. She reached out and stroked his smooth, straight blond hair —so unlike her own knotted, bird's nest—and then, trembling slightly, she took his hand.

"Where're we going, *Granmè*?" he asked, in English, except for the term of endearment.

Marie smiled.

Children knew.

They *always* knew.

So much better at understanding than adults.

She twisted the crown of the pocket watch another few notches.

And made them disappear.

Back in the corridor at the End of Time, Marie stood in the doorway, staring through to the day of the arrival of Sébastien's parents. She looked over them, the only moving parts in the whole of the otherwise still-born airport surroundings. She watched on as Sébastien rushed over to his mother and father, and ran into their arms. The wide open grins on their faces, pulling back their mouths to show off their bright, white teeth.

As Sébastien's father hauled him up into his arms, Sébastien twisted about in his father's hold, turned his head back to Marie. His eyes met hers for a fraction of a second, and he gave her one of those nervous, child's smiles.

Clench tightly in his fist, Marie saw the pocket watch, its silver casing as brightly white as Sébastien's parents' teeth. As she turned her back on the scene—returned to the gloom of the corridor at the End of Time—she wondered if Sébastien would understand what she had told him. If his six-year-old's brain had fully comprehended what she had said.

Oh, in all likelihood, when Sébastien's parents found him in possession of the watch then they would stow it somewhere safe—knowing that it couldn't rightly be returned to *Granmè* now that she lay buried beneath the rubble of her former home: the house that she had refused to leave, against all sound advice.

Would they try to bury the pocket watch with her?

Or would they keep it safe until Sébastien could understand its value?

As she allowed the darkness to wash in over her—the favour from the Administrators fully delivered as promised—she awaited what would come next; safely in the knowledge that Sébastien, like her, when the time was right, would discover the powers of the pocket watch.

So that he might explore his own worlds.

The worlds which surrounded his life:

His past.

His present.

And his *future*.

In whichever city that turned out to be.

BROTHERS OF FEAST

I T WAS MURDER to get meat sauce out of an embroidered tunic; Frankenmoore could remember his mother saying something along those lines once.

As he busied himself with the soapy water slopping free from the damp-afflicted wooden bucket, Frankenmoore swore lightly under his breath, scrubbing at the cloth with the same brush he used to pick his horse's hooves clean. It was a nightmare to so much as see his own hands in front of his face in the bleak candlelight, let alone to try and get stains out.

Warm steam puffed up into the washroom air, around the back of Sire Bvvad's castle. He felt the heat return to him at twice the strength, bouncing off the stone walls surrounding him, enticing the sweat to leak from all parts of his body. He wiped the layer of sweat from his forehead with the back of his tunic sleeve. He let out a long and hard exhale, tasting, once more, that delicious meat broth which Sire Bvvad had laid on earlier this evening for the Winter's Lights: the final large celebration of the year to which Frankenmoore, and his brother, Tildermoore, had been invited.

Frankenmoore looked down at his tunic.

If he looked at it *just so*—if he shut *one eye* and just . . . but, no, it was worthless.

Even in the candlelight it looked as if he had acquired a—*rather odd*—habit of dipping his tunic in his broth and then suckling on it. There seemed to be nothing to be done.

Frankenmoore examined the twinkling sequins, and the gold-and-silver leopard-print. The tunic, coupled with the impossibly tight lederhosen, had seemed far too extravagant for this evening. But Tildermoore had assured him that, really, he would be fine.

That—if anything—it was important that Frankenmoore *stood out* . . .

However, right now, one thing was for certain. Frankenmoore would have little chance of 'wooing' Sire Bvvad's rather fetching—and *quite blond*—daughter Neela looking as if he had lowed his head into a trough and feasted his face . . . and although that *wasn't* to say that *wasn't* the truth of what had happened, it was only good manners to pretend it wasn't the case.

At least until he had managed to persuade her father that, in actual fact, he would be the perfect suitor for Neela.

He had been sat at a wooden bench quite a distance from Neela, and the rest of her family, so he was fairly certain that if he could only dispose of—or mitigate—the evidence then he wouldn't have done his chances any harm at all. Then there would just be the normal obstacles; his ginormous frame, and waddling gait; the way that his breath smelled—*constantly*—of onions and garlic . . . and then there was his *personality* . . . how he had the habit of saying quite *outrageous* things that were clearly out of place in polite company.

But his brother, Tildermoore, had assured him that he would keep him well and truly in check.

As he resigned himself to the fact that there was nothing more to be done with his tunic—short of incinerating the *damn* thing—he gave the bucket full of soapy water a hefty kick and watched it topple over. Warm water spilled all over the stone floor, and he stared at it for the longest while, watching it lap about his boots. It reminded him of when he and his brother had been children. And their parents had taken them down to the sea.

Their father—a well-respected knight in the Lord's court—had been summoned to slay a bridge troll which happened to be lurking nearby. And their father, never one to pass up an opportunity to mix work and family, had brought them all along for the trip.

Frankenmoore could clearly recall how, when he had emerged naked from the surf, he had seen his father approaching them with his lopsided stride, his armour caked in mud, but the visor of his helmet tipped up to reveal his smiling, bronzed face within.

A good day's work.

Just as it always was.

If only Frankenmoore—or Tildermoore, for that matter—had inherited one jot of their father's ability as a knight. Still, their father's more tangible—*monetary*—inheritance had made it so that these failings were not so pronounced as they might've been otherwise.

And so Frankenmoore and Tildermoore, spurred by their father's grand old reputation, had taken to touring the nation's castles, and partaking in whichever feasts tickled their fancy; each of them looking to bring back a fair maiden to the family homestead, where their aging mother waited, day by day hopeful of an approaching wedding procession.

He had disappointed her so many times, and he was *determined* that he would disappoint her no more. By all that was Good and Holy he *would* bring home a maiden to make his mother proud!

. . . And this was where Neela fit in.

"Brother?" It was Tildermoore. "Are you quite all right in there?"

Frankenmoore turned away from the spilled bucket, glanced back over his shoulder. He caught sight of Tildermoore peering around the corner. Most days, Frankenmoore woke up cursing having found himself in the body he had. His doughy frame. His mouldy-brown, curly hair. The lashings of freckles, and acne scars beneath, which afflicted his cheeks. His brother, Tildermoore, on the other hand, had shiny, smooth—*impossibly straight*—sable hair with the chiselled features of their father. Not a freckle, or acne scar, or so much as a humble *spot*, to be found.

In addition, Tildermoore also had a washboard stomach which

Frankenmoore might've cracked horse chestnuts on . . . had he ever been so inclined. And all of these physical gifts had been presented Tildermoore without so much as a single hard day's work on his part.

It was only a minor consolation that Tildermoore was just as useless at handling himself with a sword as Frankenmoore. But, due to Tildermoore's appearance, he didn't *exactly* need to wang a sword about his head to get the ladies all aflutter.

As Tildermoore rounded the doorway, he tutted to himself. And then, with a gesture that always reminded Frankenmoore of their mother, he rested a hand on his hip and cocked his head to one side. That universal signal for disapproval. "What've you done there, Frank?" Tildermoore asked.

Frankenmoore hated how his brother made him feel like some insignificant *idiot* at any opportunity of his choosing. And although Tildermoore, more often than not, was quite correct in his disapproval, it didn't make it any less painful for Frankenmoore to bear.

Tildermoore trod closer. "Oh dear," he said, adding a shake of his head to the general stance of reproach. "You'll never get that out."

"You don't think?" Frankenmoore said, glancing up at his brother, and already scolding himself for the tone of desperation in his voice.

Tildermoore pressed his lips tightly together and gave Frankenmoore a final—*decisive*—shake of his head.

"What am I going to do? I mean, I can't go back in there, looking like this." He felt his cheeks flush slightly. "I can't ask Sire Bvvad's daughter's hand looking like this."

Tildermoore cupped his chin with his hand and tapped away at the dimple there. Some days Frankenmoore wondered if the dimple in Tildermoore's chin had come into being because of this partic-ular tick. "You're planning to marry this girl?" Tildermoore asked.

Frankenmoore felt himself blush a little harder. "No. Not *marry*. I mean, not *quite* yet, anyway . . . I thought that I'd at least *dance* with her first."

"Do you know *how* to dance?"

"Uh," Frankenmoore, stared down at the toes of his boots, then did a slight shuffle.

"Hmm," Tildermoore replied, and then, apparently shedding off the heavy atmosphere pressing down on the washroom, arched his shoulders back, drew a deep breath and then breathed it out—all over Frankenmoore.

At least Frankenmoore could honestly say that his brother's breath was just as rancid-smelling as his own.

"I *suppose* we could swap tunics," Tildermoore said.

Frankenmoore looked to his brother's chiselled body, to his athletic body.

And—*more precisely*—to the near skin-tight black tunic he wore.

But was there any other choice?

THE BANQUET HALL was really *bouncing*.

As Frankenmoore turned the corner and found himself standing on a balcony several feet above the dancefloor, he smelled the stale odour of ale on the air. On the other side of the hall, he spied the minstrels, chittering away at some ballad, or waltz, or . . . well, whatever the difference was between those styles of *music*.

The heat was something extraordinary. More extraordinary *still* was how his brother's tunic—the one which he wore—seemed to prevent him from sweating. It was as if the sweat just collected beneath the surface of the material and resided there, ready—*one fateful day*—to pop out.

His brother *always* wore black. He would be seen in nothing else.

And while Frankenmoore had often overheard rumour of black helping to 'thin' a doughy frame, he had never quite been able to believe it. To Frankenmoore it sounded a little bit too much like witchcraft. And witchcraft—as his father had often regaled him and his brother—was a Very Good Way Indeed to lose one's eyebrows. Like Frankenmoore needed any *more* physical blockades.

Though, truth be told, his eyebrows probably could do with a trim . . .

Anyway, he was here now, leaning over the brass railing of the balcony, dressed in his brother's black tunic, staring down on the mincing dancers below. As he stared down, he felt his brother sidle up beside him. And then—in that annoyingly *carefree* way of his—turn his back to the balcony and lean up against it. He produced a wooden splinter and began to pick at his teeth.

"Seen her?" Tildermoore asked.

Frankenmoore's eyes skirted the crowd, and—*sure enough*—he spotted his bride-to-be.

Neela.

Tonight she wore a mauve bodice over a floaty white rose-petal dress. Her blond hair draped down over her neck and back. Lines burrowed in around her mouth and eyes as she laughed her head off at whatever it was the Berk in Green, dancing with her, was saying.

Although his heart was rattling along at about a thousand beats a minute, Frankenmoore managed to slip his brother a fairly nonchalant glance, and say, in an even, *masculine* voice, "*Yes.*"

Tildermoore glanced casually over his shoulder, and—Frankenmoore was certain—a half dozen Fair Maidens shifted curious looks in his direction. Despite having studied Tildermoore long and hard, and over many years—*more feasts*—Frankenmoore hadn't yet discovered the secret to Tildermoore's charm. It seemed almost like something which he turned on, and which, properly adjusted, could send bodices popping of their own free will.

Was a washboard stomach really so devastating a weapon in love?

It seemed so . .

Frankenmoore turned his glance back to Neela. She and the Berk in Green had ceased their dancing for the time being and had shifted the focus of their energies to conversation.

Frankenmoore balled his fists and set them down on the brass railing. He felt the chill from the metal pass through the surface of his skin, and send the blood swilling to his head.

If only he had *something* to offer.

If only he had a *dash* of what it was his brother had.

Whereas his brother was more than content to go chasing the proverbial tail about the courts of the land, Frankenmoore had told himself—*from Day One, no less*—that he would be entirely content to bag himself a wife once and for all.

Let Tildermoore keep up his never-ending flirtations and saucy encounters.

All that Frankenmoore really aspired to obtain was a Fair—and, all things being equal, *compliant*—Maiden whom he could take home to meet his mother.

With whom his mother would be *quite* contented.

Was that too much to ask?

"Come on, then," Tildermoore said, grabbing hold of the front of Frankenmoore's tunic, and dragging him away from the edge of the balcony. "Let's go *get* her."

3

DOWN ON THE DANCEFLOOR—consisting of rather pleasant, if not slightly *clichéd*, black-and-white tiles—Frankenmoore felt his anxiety reaching its peak.

The hot bodies swung back and forth, moving as swiftly as they were befuddling. Even as he felt himself pulled along in his brother's wake, he did his best to attempt to comprehend the beleaguering foot placements, the elaborate hand movements . . . and the bouts of laughter from the pairs of dancers—as if there was something *humorous* about this whole sorry façade!

He might well have toppled over and landed with a *thud* on the dancefloor, down among the stomping feet, and the pungent perfumes, and the poorly concealed odour of flatulence . . . but his brother, perhaps sensing his growing anxieties, grabbed him by the wrist and dragged him onward.

Through the crowd.

Before he really knew what hit him, he found himself in the vicinity of Neela and the Berk in Green. The two of them—just like the rest of the dancers—twirling back and forth, apparently greatly *enjoying* the experience. Although he would've liked nothing more than to retreat from the—apparently happy—couple, his brother continued to tug him forth, toward the two of them.

There was no doubt in his mind that it had been a real mistake.

That this was a *huge* mistake.

Over the scratching music and the *blabber* of the dancers, he observed Tildermoore tapping the Berk in Green on the shoulder, leaning into him. And then he overheard Tildermoore's belly laugh, and read the gaping features of the Berk in Green. With a strangely bitter-sweet feeling, Frankenmoore watched on as the Berk in Green untangled his fingers from Neela's, looked right through the bundled-up people, for a second staring into Frankenmoore's eyes, then appearing to turn slightly pale. When he glanced back at Neela, he gave her something of a *squiffy* look and then retreated off through the crowd of dancers.

Not looking back once.

Frankenmoore just stood still—*stunned*—not quite able to believe what had happened. When Tildermoore glanced over his shoulder, looked back to him, Frankenmoore felt his chest tightening. There was a sharp tingling sensation in his ribcage . . . not unrelated to the extremely close-fitting tunic of his brother's he now wore. Tildermoore gave him a 'come-hither' gesture and Frankenmoore knew there was nothing he would be able to do to resist.

With a swift—and fairly *vain*—glance about the Banquet Hall, Frankenmoore caught sight of Sire Bvvad on the platform raised above the crowd. Quite unlike the dour, sombre presence the man had been earlier. When he had greeted Frankenmoore and his brother at the entrance to his castle his mouth had appeared like a cat's pinched anus; a look with which Frankenmoore was well-acquainted, it seemed to be the prevailing one whenever their footman announced them . . . such was the reputation of those of *inherited* wealth. Now, however, Sire Bvvad's cheeks were reddened, and his eyelids were droopy. He danced with thin air, trailing an invisible partner about in his arms in time to the music—or, well, Frankenmoore was *fairly* certain it was 'in time'.

It was quite clear, even without his brother's intervention, that Sire Bvvad had other *intangible* things on his mind apart from the fate of his daughter at the present moment.

"*Brother!*"

Frankenmoore turned in the direction of Tildermoore and Neela.

Quite to his surprise, he realised that the two of them were grinning at him. He found the spectacle somewhat infectious. Before he could catch himself, he was grinning back. Taking strides through the crowded-up dancers to reach them.

When he arrived at their side, he breathed in Neela's heady perfume—a kind of mixture of honey and silk . . . did silk *have* a smell? . . . with that ever-so feminine scent of *horse* thrown in for good measure: the daughters of well-heeled knights often did spend their many—*many*—leisure hours in the company of horses.

"Brother!" Tildermoore barked again, once Frankenmoore was closer.

In truth, the word almost deafened Frankenmoore.

"Allow me to present you to, the quite fetching, and quite *scandalous*"—here Tildermoore leaned in and offered Neela a secretive glance; Neela gave a twinkle-eyed grin in reply—"daughter of Sire Bvvad, our host for the evening."

Before Frankenmoore could truly get his head around just what was happening, he felt Tildermoore transfer Neela's delicate—and oddly *bony*—hand over to him. He felt her fragile fingertips brush against the fleshy part of his palm.

He felt her heartbeat!

And her body warmth!

To begin with, he could hardly contain himself enough to realise she was speaking to him—that she *had* spoken to him. It was all he could do to lean into her, and to say, "*Wha*?" at the top of his voice.

Neela gave his hand a squeeze and leaned in closer, over the top of his—quite *fleshy*—shoulder. He felt her warm breath up against his earlobe, mitigated only by the icy-cool tone of her voice. "Your brother!" she shouted. "He tells me you're quite the horseman!"

"Uh," Frankenmoore found himself replying without so much as a thought skittering through his head. Quickly, he glanced around and was unsurprised to discover that Tildermoore had made himself scarce. He turned back to Neela. Tried his best to put on a good smile. "Yes, that's right."

Her eyes sparkled. She squeezed his hand again. "What say you that we get away from here and I show you the stables?"

He felt his eyeballs near enough bulge out of their sockets. He gaped around the Banquet Hall, his focus coming to rest once again on Sire Bvvad, who had now descended from his previous state—the dancing back and forth with an invisible partner—to sitting, knees hunched up to his chest, eyes closed, and finger waggling through the air, apparently believing himself to be conducting the musicians.

"Don't worry about my father," she replied. "He was a *great* knight once, but as you can see"—she gestured to him through the dancers as if he hadn't yet thoroughly pinned him—"he much prefers the company of his flagon to his *daughter* these days."

Despite himself, he couldn't help but reply, "No son?"

Here she narrowed her eyes, made her lips pert and replied, "No."

4

FRANKENMOORE wasn't quite sure what he had imagined *exactly* when he had envisioned the ideal Fair Maiden, but he *was* fairly certain that he hadn't believed she would be anything like this.

He had anticipated a somewhat romantic scene in the stables. Neela introducing him to her *many* fair fillies, while Frankenmoore imitated his brother, resting his fingertips in the dimple in his chin that simply didn't exist, *Hmming* and *Ahhing* before they retired to her bed chambers, or—failing that—took a midnight walk through the gardens.

However, Neela, it turned out, had other plans.

As he stood in the chilly night air of the stables, he breathed in the scent of urinated hay set to a soundtrack of whinnies. He could still taste the broth at the back of his throat, although the flavour was becoming more and more distant with each passing minute. In his wildest of fantasies, he wondered if Neela might lead him to the kitchen for a midnight feast once they got done with ravishing one another's bodies.

Not so.

In fact, at the present moment, Neela stood before him—*all action*—dressed in her riding cloak, having ditched her ball gown, busying herself with the bolt to one of the stable doors.

"Ah—" he said, deciding he needed to take action here, but Neela cut him off before he'd even got started.

"Your brother said you've killed more than a thousand men."

He felt his stomach knot. He tried his best to form words, but they simply wouldn't come.

Neela continued, without halting. "That's good," she said,

"because I'm going to need a big—*tough*—man who's not afraid to split skulls for my getaway."

"Your 'getaway' ?" Frankenmoore said, watching on as Neela produced a golden steed from around the stable. He was a little taken aback by the sheer *size* of the thing, and he never would've believed that Neela would be able to haul herself up onto its back without his assistance.

However, after clambering her way up onto the top of the stable door, she took a leap and landed neatly—one leg either side of the horse's flanks—in a masculine posture.

He noticed how she hadn't so much as bothered to put a saddle on the horse, or a bridle, for that matter. In truth, he had never been the greatest of horse riders. Quite frankly, he could do with all the help he could get.

"Come on, then!" Neela said, jerking her head back at the stables, to another of the doors. "You can take your pick—my father won't mind, by this point in the evening he will be seeing the world in *twos* . . . he'll think he has *twice* the horses he actually does."

Without another thought, he found himself replying, "Like witchcraft."

"Uh-huh," she said, responding to the nasal stirrings of her steed, and, gripping tight to its mane, leading it in a series of calming circles.

He glanced back to the castle.

It loomed up and out from the night, its torches shining their orange light all around. He could see a scattering of lazy guards up on the ramparts, crossbows hoisted over their shoulders, some with sabres hanging from their waistlines. He was already estimating just how many seconds he would manage to survive against one of those —*apparently extremely competent*—swordsmen.

As he deliberated mortality—among other things—Neela leaned down from her steed and said, in a whisper, "Come on, get a move on, before the guards see you."

He took the decision over his mount surprisingly quickly. Not wanting to seem like he didn't know what he was doing, he glanced in casually to the first couple of stables, pouting as he did so, before finally—though not with any great enthusiasm—settling on the horse within.

He worked quickly, unbolting the door—that part wasn't too strenuous—before entering the stable itself. And finding himself confronting the looming silhouette of a dozing horse, glaring at him suspiciously from out of a half-opened eye.

Neela gave him another hurried whisper. "*Quickly*! There's a *guard* coming!"

It was as if she had known him his entire life—she knew *exactly* what to say to kick him out of inaction. Moving fast, he rounded the horse, glanced at it once—*twice*—and then, hearing a distant shout, grabbed hold of the mane and tried his best to haul himself up onto its back.

Of course he *couldn't*.

On the best of days—sunny skies, gentle breeze, etcetera, etcetera—Frankenmoore could just about hoist himself onto a *well-saddled* horse with the aid of an overturned crate, or—*better*—a boost-up from one of their footmen. But—*dammit!*—Roger was nowhere to be seen, and being *lifted* onto the horse would be hardly fitting with the romantic image his brother had conjured. Which was to say nothing of the guards, and their pointed objects, approaching at a rapid click.

No, he was determined.

He *had* to get himself up onto this horse's back.

No way around it.

Mind made up, he used all the strength he could muster to haul his—*sizeable*—weight up off the floor of the stable. There was a moment when he was fairly certain he had managed it; that he *was* going to get up onto the horse's back after all.

Unfortunately, though, that moment was really quite short lived.

Right at the second when he heard the *bark* of one of the guards calling out, "Who goes there?!" he felt the horse kick its hooves, apparently having taken note of the open stable door. He could only think to cling tight to the horse's mane as it cantered out through the gap—his feet dragging along the stone cobbles as it went.

For a fraction of a second, he found himself eye to eye with a guard—and his flared nostrils—but his hold on the horse's mane was *unshifting* and *sure*, and the horse broke into a gallop, taking the two of them away from the guards at a fast pace.

Before he had quite gathered what was going on, he felt the ground soften, felt the chill of a muddy sod fling up and strike him on the cheek.

And then another.

Another followed. And then several more.

He closed his eyes for the majority of the 'ride', until he sensed the horse slowing to a more gentle—but oddly *far from* relaxing —pace.

When he did open his eyes, he found that the castle was now off on the horizon, only the blaze of the torches marking it out from the darkness. Once his brain could deal with the background, he turned his attention to his more immediate surroundings. They had arrived to a forest, on the edge of Sire Bvvad's lands. The very forest which he, and his brother, had taken great pains to avoid.

In accordance with the motto they had shared for the length of their—*comparatively long*—lives:

Don't go looking for trouble . . .

As the chattering of pine martins—or was that the sound of bandits sharpening their scimitars?—sounded in his ears, Frankenmoore glanced about for Neela.

Finally, he found her.

She sat quite upright—*quite proud*—upon her steed.

She gave him a smirk. "Well," she said, "you're looking quite a state."

As if he didn't understand what she was going on about, he reached up and touched his cheek. Realised that, as she implied, his face was caked in mud . . . in fact, as his hands searched further south, he noted that his tunic—*too*—was caked in mud.

Tildermoore would be furious.

"You can let go of the horse now," she added.

He looked to the horse's mane, and to where he clung to it. He realised that he could no longer feel his hands, that his fingers had quite simply frozen in place. As if his body was only just now catching onto what was happening, he felt a tingle pass over the surface of his skin.

He released the mane.

And tumbled down onto the sodden earth.

When he turned his attention upward, back to Neela, her smirk seemed to have widened. He decided that if he was going to ask the question, then it needed to be now. That he most likely wouldn't get another chance. "My lady, will you take my hand in marriage?"

Neela's smirk slid off her lips, and her eyes wandered onto his. She frowned long and hard, clearly considering the request. Then, finally, she said, "Not bloody likely—I've a *rather rugged* rogue waiting in there for me," and tugged on her horse's mane and cantered off into the forest.

Frankenmoore lay there, on his side, in the muddy, mossy earth at the entrance to the forest.

On the horizon, he made out the gentle, pinkish glow of the

rising sun. He thought a lot about life, and how it had brought him here, to this precise moment. And then, quite soon after he had begun thinking about it, he stopped.

There was nothing noble about giving your sense of self-worth a *real* kicking when it was down.

STRANGER IN THE HILLS

I

T HE GRAVEL CRUNCHED beneath Tine's feet as he made his way down the path into the village, clutching the still-warm loaf of bread to his chest, still wrapped in its paper bag. That sweet smell, the cinnamon and raisins baked into it all wafted up his nostrils, and he just couldn't wait to get the bread home—the looks on his family's faces, the rosiness in their cheeks as he brought this back for them. His mouth salivated at the prospect of the tea and bread, with fresh butter and jam smothered across the top. Just what he needed to warm up on a chilly day like this.

As Tine dodged several larger rocks, taking care not to trip over and clutching the bread tighter as he went, he observed the snow-capped mountains in the distance, and then the lower foothills which hung over the village. All was set in the moonlight. There was just so much space. Sometimes he found it overwhelming to be out here, all alone. He'd just gone past his fifteenth birthday, just got out of school and gone to work in the next village over. And so he'd never experienced this, being out here just with his thoughts.

He reached the end of the gravel path and the beginnings of the cobblestones, the start of his village. He stared out across the crooked rooftops, the jagged walls, all white-washed with thatched roofs. He could never imagine going away from here, going and living somewhere else.

This place—his home—it was his idea of perfection.

Just as he came level with the first house of the village, he stepped more lightly. He hadn't much interest in getting the owner out—an elderly man who had wispy shock-white hair and jug ears. He always brandished a cane, waggling it about over him as if he was just looking for some unsuspecting person to bring it down on.

Tine could hear his own breathing, his tunic rising and falling

41

against his chest as he went. He fixed his eyes on the old man's house, willing him not to come out—to shout at him and chase him off down the street. It was strange because the old man would never catch him. Although the man had never shown him anything but rage, he never wished to cause him harm or to stoke his fire at all. The man was clearly old, troubled, and in need of someone to look after him—if only he would allow someone close.

Tine cleared the house, its rickety fenced garden, and proceeded on down into the heart of the village. The bread had cooled a little now and he had to really clutch it tight to his chest to get any remnant of the warmth into him. The smell too was disappearing, now he was unsure whether he really smelled what he smelled or if it was just a memory.

Just like always at this time of night, the village centre was deserted. The bronze statue which occupied the centre of the town —a rugged man holding a hoe up to the sky, with a woman and child huddled down beside him. As he always did upon passing the statue, he reached out and rubbed the man's lucky left knee, and then, like all boys of his age, he supposed, he lingered a long time on the woman's cleavage, the flesh-like bronze lumps which were squashed up against her blouse.

He almost slipped up on a patch of donkey manure, on his way up to his house. He listened to the *squelch* as his boot sank into it. He wiped his boot up against a tuft of grass which grew between the cobblestones, wincing a little at the harsh smell that filled his mouth, seemed to dampen his tongue. And then, feeling his boots a little damp from the manure, he headed onward, already eyeing his front door.

He noticed the smile growing on his face, the heat returning to his cheeks, as he reached out to turn the doorknob, already that warmth, the wood-burning stove, the slightly annoying twin pecks his mother would give him on either cheek, and the inevitable wrestle with his younger brothers. And then, with his arm outstretched, resting on the doorknob, he felt a shiver run up his neck, all around his collar. He turned around and looked behind him.

There, up there, in the foothills leading up to the mountain, he saw a man on horseback. He absorbed him, squinting in the moonlight. The man wore all black and he sat straight-backed on the horse, apparently staring right at Tine.

Normally, as was the custom in the village, and the next village over where Tine worked, he would've greeted the man, but this time, no. Just something otherworldly, something deep-set and survival-orientated told him to get away. To go inside and forget that he'd ever seen anyone. He listened to the *rustle* of the bread's paper bag in his hand and that seemed to return sense to him. And then, just as he turned the doorknob a touch, he heard the unmistakable *clop* of hooves against the cobblestones, that smell of warmed-horse hide, and before he knew it the horse and rider were standing right over him, that warm, rancid-smelling breath of the horse blowing against his cheek.

The horse and rider seemed impossibly high, standing beside him. And Tine had to crane his neck to get any sort of look at the stranger who sat up there, in the saddle. The stranger wore a hood so that his face was covered. That sense, that tingling chill rose a few notches, and Tine gripped the doorknob tighter, everything telling him to turn away, to slip back inside. And he would've done just that if only the stranger hadn't addressed him.

"Good evening," he said.

A lump formed in Tine's throat, he felt his hands shaking, that warm horse sweat clinging to his nostrils. But he got the words out eventually. "Good evening, sir."

"I'm a traveller," the man said. "I'm just passing through here, and I wondered, ah"—the man paused for several moments, searching for the expression—"if you would lead me to . . . well, it's a house—a large house, near here, I think."

Despite the overwhelming chill, the way that his mouth seemed impossibly dry, and his tongue like a soaked sponge, Tine managed to respond. "Yes," he said, nodding as he spoke. "There is a large house, at least, of the large houses I think I know which one you mean. Yes, I know of a large house."

"But would you take me there?"

Tine glanced up and down the street, just hoping someone else might be around, that he might be able to fob the stranger off on someone else. As it was he knew that he couldn't possibly go with this man, it was better that he just go inside. Right now. He turned the doorknob and felt it give way, and then, impossibly, it turned back against him. Not with excessive force, but just enough so that it felt jammed. He wished to cry out but his throat had become so constricted, his heart was beating so fast, that he just couldn't summon the will. He found himself staring up, the whole form dark, face in shadow, all except those beady eyes—inky black and gleaming in the moonlight—staring down at him.

"Please," the stranger said. "I would make it worth your while."

An object flipped up into the air and landed on the cobblestones with a tinny *tinkle*.

A coin.

If Tine hadn't been so afraid he would've been offended. Just who did this man think that he was—some beggar praying for scraps? He was a carpenter, an apprentice, but he dreamed that one day he would have his own shop, and he would craft wonderful things. And yet his thoughts were blank, and his lips parted wide in empty awe.

When the stranger spoke again it seemed that there was a smile in his voice. "If you show me what I want to see I promise there'll be more from where that came from."

The bread was stone cold now, and any dreams of that jam, that butter, the warmth of the tea, was a long-forgotten memory. It was like someone had scooped out his innards and left him an empty, cold chamber. And yet he was afraid. What might this stranger do if he said no? His family were inside his house here and, this man, he just stank of copper . . . death.

"What do you say?" the stranger said, still sounding calm.

"Okay," Tine replied, setting the bread down on the doorstep.

2

T HE STRANGER HELPED Tine onto the horse, dragging him up and helping him secure himself onto the saddle behind him. The leather felt hard beneath Tine's bottom and he struggled to settle. He was glad the stranger didn't make any comment about whether he'd ever ridden a horse before—but to tell the truth Tine hadn't much, it was just that everything was in walking distance from his home. His family had never needed one. Everything they needed was right here.

The horse held a sturdy, sure gait, its body plodding along, apparently not much bothered to be carrying two riders instead of one. Now that Tine was perched on top of its back, the smell—that dry, *hairy* smell—was stronger and he had the urge to sneeze. Each steady *clop* was accompanied by a saunter to the left or the right from the horse, and in that way they carried on through the village.

The stranger spoke to him over his shoulder. From the way he spoke Tine could tell clearly that he was a foreigner. Although he spoke Tine's language well, with lots of words Tine had heard only once or twice from doctors or priests, he could tell that the stranger was out of practice with the language. He wondered to himself where the stranger might be from. But didn't dare ask.

"This house," the stranger said. "What does it look like exactly?"

"Well," Tine said, racking his brains—he'd never been that good at describing things, he was better with his hands: give him a block of wood and he would sculpt whatever the image in his mind was. "It's kind of big. You know, with great boxy shapes to it. There's the front porch with a large wooden frame, and then it just goes up and up and up."

The stranger remained silent and Tine took this as a prompt

that whatever job he was doing at describing the place it was adequate.

"And there's a great big garden around it, a bit of a mess now, though."

"Is there anyone living there?"

"I don't think so."

The horse's hooves clopped along and they slipped into silence. They left the village behind, climbing through the foothills, into the maze of paths which Tine knew so well, but also knew that a stranger would lose themselves in in an instant. The chill seemed to subside slightly and Tine felt the more familiar, fresher—with somehow more . . . living warmth—of the breeze coming down off the snowy mountains. Although he shuddered it warmed him inside, made him feel back alive, pushing back that deathly sensation that seemed to lurk over this stranger.

He tasted that cold, that living, breathing cold. And it refreshed him all over again.

They trod on, through the crevice in the rock which Tine indicated. The horse's steps quickened and Tine felt a touch uneasy again, he grasped the back of the saddle beneath his bottom and clung on. He glanced over the stranger's shoulder in the direction they headed. Soon the house would come into view. Soon they would . . .

The horse emerged from between the rock and down below, spread out before them, was the house, just as Tine had described it. Now, in the moonlight, there was something ghastly about it, something that suggested to Tine that it just shouldn't be there. Looking at it, Tine had always felt a touch uncomfortable but now he truly felt that it was a scar on the landscape, a blister on the otherwise pristine countryside valley. He wished, more than anything, to get down off the horse and go off back home. He estimated it at a half an hour's walk, an hour at most, he could be back there, at home—all that warmth, the familiarity of his mother and brothers.

That all seemed so distant out here, with this stranger.

As if the wind had caught his thoughts, a sudden and chillier gale blew, sending his hair fluttering all around his face, getting caught in his eyes and mouth, and he caught the musky scent of the stranger—this traveller—and he didn't doubt that he had been travelling for days at a time, that he was ragged and ready to rest.

It seemed the horse shared his thoughts as it suddenly came to a stop, rearing its head upward. The stranger clucked his tongue several times and jerked on the reins, but it was clear that the horse wouldn't go any further. The stranger hunched his shoulders and then glared down into the valley, to the house. He turned around to Tine and said, "I'll tie the horse up here and we'll go down there by foot."

Tine, at this point, what with the goose flesh breaking out all over him, the wind picking up so that it whistled through the rocks behind them and sending the tree branches creaking, decided that this was as far as he would go. Feeling a little more sure of himself, more assured that he could speak clearly with the stranger, he said, "I said that I'd show you to the house and I've done that—now can I go back home, to the village?"

The stranger breathed long and hard. He breathed out moist clouds thick with a stench of tobacco. And then, as if the stranger had answered Tine's question, hail began to fall. It chattered all around them as it landed on the hard ground—it reminded Tine of falling fruit. It stung his skin as it hit and he found himself, without a chance to respond to the stranger, already barrelling down the hill, accompanying him, both of them headed for the house.

THE STRANGER HAD A KEY, and he let them in through the towering garden gate, into the sprawling garden and then, the two of them running to escape the hail, up to the front porch of the house. Tine hadn't much time to get a look at the exterior, to compare it to how he had stored it in memory, but he saw now, from the brief glimpses he got on the way, that it was sprawling, all iron railings and jet-black windows—like mirrors. They arrived on the doorstep where, with a faint *jangle* of a keychain, the stranger brought another key to bear on the lock. And then, just like that, the two of them were standing inside the house, gloom all around them, the smell of damp smothering everything. Hail rattled against the roof, spilling like loosed beads down the exterior walls and pattering to a halt in the overgrown grass outside.

A staircase opened up before Tine, and he glanced up it. Another shudder passed through him, that same hollowness was returning. And he knew that now there would be no escape from the feeling—not unless he wished to run outside, to catch his death running back to the village in the hailstorm.

The stranger's steps echoed all around, the woody *thunk* of his boots across the floors. He reached into his overcoat and produced a match, which he struck into a flame. Shielding the flame with his hand, he shone it on his immediate surroundings, straight away locating a candlestick nearby, standing proud in the hallway. He stepped over to it and lit the candle. The flame grew steadier, more consistent. And at last Tine had a chance to take in this place.

There were oil paintings on the walls, dozens of scenes with mulchy browns, and mouldy greens, none of it appealed to Tine, but he had no idea what rich people had in mind when they talked about taste. Of the few rich people he had known he had never been able to come up with an appropriate comment to make on things such as these—the *finer* things as they might say.

The candlelight laid Tine's nerves to rest to an extent, and he felt his body once more warm, and he dared to shuck off the uneasiness clenching his bones tight, telling him to run.

The stranger headed on through the house and, not wanting to be left behind, even in the well-lit hallway, Tine followed the man. As the stranger carried onward, he brought his hood down, letting it rest against his shoulders. Tine stalked along behind him, hoping to get a view of his face, at least in profile. But the darkness seeped in, growing all around them, and soon all that he could make out were shapes—the basic forms of things—in the scraps of light from the candle back in the hall.

All at once, Tine noted, the hail stopped. The *pitter-patter* on the roof tiles ceased. And, after a couple more drops of hail, there was complete silence in the house. Only the sound of their respiration, and the light *crackle* of the flame back in the hall.

Tine bumped into something, his knee making contact with something soft yet rigid. Blind in the darkness, he felt before him and found his fingertips coming into contact with the coarse material. He shifted his touch along the frame of the object. An armchair. He continued his blind exploration, working his fingers upward and then he reached something which felt leathery and stiff, out of place. Not part of the armchair. He was about to call out to the stranger that he had found something, something strange, and then, just as the word rested on his tongue, ready to leave his lips, another match sparked up—the stranger much closer than he ever would've imagined—and that same unsteady glow shod all over the scene. What Tine was looking at—what he was touching—it was nothing less than a person.

A *dead* person.

4

TINE STUMBLED BACK, his arms flailing, trying to make contact with something that might support him, stop him simply falling right onto the ground. But nothing came handy and he tumbled down, falling on those hard, wooden floorboards with a loud *thud*.

The stranger, still holding the match in his hand, had apparently not noticed Tine's reaction to the corpse, and he held his head out, stretching his neck to take it all in. His eyes, they were like obsidian, so black as to be mistaken for a bird's eyes—not human at all. He had jagged cheekbones and slick hair, as black as his eyes. Now Tine realised that he had stood with a hunch previously—why, he had no idea—and that he was actually a towering, virile specimen, much younger than he had anticipated, certainly not older than thirty.

Tine drew breath and felt it squeak in his throat. He noted the body now, was able to take it in more fully and with, not calm, but at least something just below total hysteria. The face was gaunt, of course, its mouth open in what appeared to be an ever-lasting scream, blackness of the mouth just as black as the stranger's eyes. The skin was chapped, cracked up and . . . as it had felt against his fingers, like untreated leather. The arms were stiff and gripped the arms of the chair in an everlasting, deathly grip.

Tine felt the rapid heartbeats all patter away in his throat and he tried to calm himself, but all he could feel was that chill—the chill from outside—descending over him again.

The stranger snapped his gaze to Tine, that same intensity with which he viewed the body.

A thousand different myths flooded through Tine's mind—all those tales that his mother, and grandmother before her, had told him about the variety of spirits that haunted these hills, the various characters. But, this man, was he . . . could he be, just like what she'd described?

And then the smell hit him. Like leather but with a sour stench attached to it—that odour which told Tine that it was unnatural, that it was an unclean state for a human, and it communicated one thing and one thing only.

Danger.

That he had to get away.

He stumbled back up, to his feet, backing up, heading out of the room, back to that glow in the hallway which was somewhat familiar compared to the horrors he had just witnessed here, which still stood before him.

His breaths came short and quick, insufficient to keep his brain from swirling around, and yet more than enough to draw the stench of the damp and the dead body deep into his lungs. He knocked up against a wall, feeling the peeling paper against his palms, and he stumbled on, arriving back in the hallway.

Only when he reached the door did he risk a glance back, over his shoulder, to where he could just about make out the vague shape of the stranger, still lingering over that body, the steady light from the match not quite enough to be able to pick out any other features.

Tine hesitated, impossibly, waiting for something. All at once everything was so placid and unmoving. He recalled a time, about a year before, when he'd been on his way back from the carpenter's shop. It was around the turn of autumn into winter, and the air smelled of rain, he could feel the hairs on his arms damp with the humidity, and he was sure he could hear the distant echoes of thunder. And yet, right before him, there was a stillness to everything. Nothing around him moved. Then, all at once, it all split open, as sure and swift as an axe blade sliced through a log.

And the storm had broken.

He returned to the present, that still scene before him, the stranger still standing over the body—the *dead* body. It reminded Tine, in a way, of how the stray dogs would sniff at spilled beer or smashed eggs, rounding the substance before bending down and lapping it up.

Feeling a quiver pass through his heart, Tine watched on as the stranger straightened up, eyes closed, hands clasped over his chest, as if he were concentrating on his own heartbeat, and then, all at once, a shadow formed itself, a few feet above the dead body, as if the deceased man's soul was peeling itself out of his skin. And it rose, up into the air, and propped itself up on its two legs.

The air turned from that light chill to an all-out freeze.

Tine's whole body, too, clenched tight, refusing to allow his will to manipulate it anymore—it was as if it had decided that now Tine had had his chance to run, and now that he had refused to follow that urge he was condemned to suffer this.

Although Tine couldn't make out the form, the facial features, or even the shape of the shadow's body, he assumed this, in some way, to be the man's . . . what? . . . soul? He watched on as the shadow bent and flexed, like a cat waking after an afternoon nap.

And now, from what Tine could make out, the stranger, still with his eyes clasped shut, was mouthing something to the shadow —conversing with him in tones that Tine just couldn't hear, even in the relative silence of the house. Against his will and his deepest thoughts, he found himself creeping back toward the stranger, drawing closer, trying to hear the words passing between the two.

Tine stooped down, afraid that the stranger might snap around in a moment and confront him, but the stranger remained fixated on his conversation with this . . . this shadow.

Tine tracked the rises and falls of the conversation, as if

watching two people speak through a window from the other side of the village. They spoke in placid tones, impossibly placid tones.

And then that same urge returned to Tine, that he had to run.

Now was his chance.

The hail had stopped.

He had to go.

And so, feeling a creeping sense of dread clasp hold of his throat, and feeling his forearm clatter into a wooden cornice of the wall, he ran back into the hallway, steeling himself in the candlelight before tracking out through the front door and into the night.

Even through his boots he wagered he could feel the cold sting of the hail stones, lying there nestled in the long grass, and he could smell that damp—from the house—clinging to his clothes. He thought back to the bread, the once-warm bread, and his mouth salivated at the prospect. Soon he would be away from here, back home, the stranger forgotten.

Tine dared not twist around and gaze back at the house as he climbed the hill, not pausing a second to catch his breath, and, up ahead, he saw the horse standing in the crevice in the rock, sheltered from the storm. As Tine passed by hurriedly, the horse regarded him with blank eyes . . . no, black eyes, just as black and beady as the stranger's.

Just as Tine reached the other end of the crevice he found himself turning, knowing now that he was safe, that there was no way the stranger could catch up with him. And he found himself, as he looked back over his shoulder, near enough blinded by the light.

Flames licked up the sides of the house, flushing the whole place with oranges and yellows, unbelievably bright against the dour night gloom. He thought he could feel the warmth, even from here, smell the woody scent of the smoke carried on the breeze. Almost unconsciously, Tine touched the rock beside him, feeling its porous dips and rough surface, needing something sure to hold onto.

Tine eyed the horse, as if expecting it to react in some way, to its master being trapped down there, in the house on fire. He brushed his tongue against his lower lip, burrowed it in the dried callouses, the taste of sawdust which stuck there no matter how much soap he lathered all over his face. And so, with the *crackle* of the flames from the house nagging away in his ears, he left the scene, running on, back toward the village.

5

TINE LISTENED to the echo of his footsteps bounce off the passing houses, return to him in such a way that he was sure that he could hear the *clop* of hooves hot on his heels. And yet, when he did dare look back over his shoulder, there was nothing— no one—there.

And why would there be?

The stranger, he had been caught in that house, most likely trapped inside. Dead. The worst part of it all was that Tine found himself wishing, hoping, that that was the case. The man—the stranger—whatever it was that he had been doing had been *unnatural*, unseen. Things like that should never happen. He knew that and wished its memory gone from his mind.

That night, after a brief scolding from his mother, he crawled into bed, hauling the scratchy blanket over his head to muffle his silent sobs. When his brother came in, to take up the bed beside him, Tine listened to the sound of his breathing, as he stood there, no doubt looking down at him.

For a long moment Tine was terrified that his brother would ask him what was wrong—why he was crying. But, to Tine's relief, his brother just sank down in his own bed, turned on his side and went to sleep.

During the next day Tine found himself distracted, unable to concentrate on his work. He sanded edges, feeling the rough woodcuts against his fingertips. But when he tried to smell, to breathe in that reassuring, familiar, woody smell, he found his senses stripped —and it smelled more like ash than fresh-cut wood. And then he was thinking about the house all over again.

Although the carpenter, Tine's employer, surely noted his absentmindedness, he made no comment—in the same way, Tine thought, that his brother had thought it better to leave him alone, not to offer any comment on his sobbing the night before. Tine was relieved when the time came to leave, to take the walk back to his village—glad to have the opportunity to clear his head with fresh, mountain air.

But the air was singed forever, and all he could taste was that same ash. He kept thinking he could see, just peeking up over the hilltops, the flames forever rising. He imagined arriving back at his village to see the place aflame. He was so swept up with the idea that, almost of themselves, he felt his feet skitter out from beneath him, increasing their pace, as if he could already hear the *crackle* of flames, and the *snap* and collapse of wooden beams.

When he got back home, of course, the place was still standing —and there was no sign of the flames creeping their way up the hill. But, even standing outside his door in the steady twilight, he knew that he couldn't go in. Not yet. He needed to return to the house.

To see the place for himself.

And so, with the quiver of hunger clasping his stomach tight, making it quiver and gurgle, he crept up the hillside, using the rocks to help his sleepy feet upward, to that same crevice he had led the stranger through the night before.

Perhaps he had expected the horse to still be there, to be rocking from side to side, both with anxiety and thirst, and Tine told himself that he would've brought the poor creature back down into the village—it wasn't *its* fault that its master was *damned*.

But the horse wasn't there.

Tine glanced down to see the stirred-up dirt, the hundreds of imprinted hoof marks where the horse had stood the night before. And then he turned to look down into the valley, where the house had stood.

The place was nothing more than a pile of cinders now. He observed the smoke still curling up from the remainders before it evaporated into the evening gloom. That ash—that same ash he had smelled back at work—still clung to the scene, and Tine wondered if, years from now, it would still be the same, if this place would be forever scarred by what he had witnessed the night before.

Because it had been nothing short of raising the dead . . . hadn't it?

Tine felt peace descend over him, a sense of relief that—until he had taken in the scene right now—he'd never thought he would have again. And then, as he turned on his heel, headed back down into the village, back to his mother's warm, hearty, meaty broth—accompanied by the remnants of the bread he had brought the day before—he caught a glint in the nascent moonlight, there down on the floor.

He stooped over and examined the item.

The coin—the same one the stranger had offered him. But how had it got here? He would have imagined it still between a pair of cobblestones, outside his house, he hadn't thought to pick it up then. And then a shudder passed through him as he thought of how the stranger might've returned to his home the night before, retrieved the coin and brought it here.

Tine stared at it for a long while, even reached out to touch it.

But he couldn't.

He just couldn't.

And before he had even consciously settled to leave it there, he found his feet already carrying him back down the hillside, down to his village, where the steady, warm glow of the orange lights welcomed him, drew him back in with open arms.

Away from all this nastiness.

WOUND BACK BELLS

I

THE MULTI-COLOURED NEONS that flickered and blinked along the pinewood shelves behind the bar were just as nauseating as they were necessary.

Green, and yellow, and purple, and blue, and orange, and some other colours that Q'oorth—being a gargoyle—quite frankly just didn't want to think about.

There was, of course, that old adage that went about the gargoyle community that rang something along the lines of 'It's not easy being grey.' Original, it was not, but, as with most clichés, it just happened to be so mundane that it was often true. Because life, for Q'oorth, at least, wasn't at all easy being grey. Not when the rest of the world ran on bright colours.

Life being grey meant blending in with the background, almost never being noticed by anything—Mortal or otherwise. Q'oorth's more conservative gargoyle friends would often claim that being noticed was hugely overrated. Easy for them to say. They didn't think he'd noticed how often they took pride in scaring away the pigeons that attempted to build nests in their horns.

Getting shat on was the high price of being disappeared in this modern world.

The other gargoyles had pride, of course they had.

They wanted to be noticed just as much as Q'oorth himself truly did.

The only difference between them and Q'oorth was that Q'oorth had the good grace to admit it. To rake up another cliché: 'honesty'—as his father, or whatever creature had brought him into being all those centuries ago had said—was its own reward.

Q'oorth let loose a stony sigh and glared down into his wooden flagon of brandy ale. It was a frothy mess, but at least, even this, the most ordinary of drinks, still had an interesting, amber-like shade to it. He glanced about.

Tonight he was all alone. The slightly campily named bar: Merv's Mythical Myre, was empty.

Other than Q'oorth and Merv, of course.

In the land of mythical creatures it was frowned upon to ask too many questions of one's origins or racial makeup, and though Q'oorth was perhaps more forthright than most, he didn't see it as his MO to tip the apple cart on that front. Though he often found himself getting his thoughts wet with those murky depths. On several occasions, in fact.

Merv, it had to be admitted, was certainly interesting. And considering that 'interesting' was a fairly standard reaction to anything spread out within the Kingdom of the Mythical Beasts, it was perhaps better to further that with the qualifier that Merv was *eyebrow-archingly* interesting.

Q'oorth loosely thought of Merv as a bird, though a flightless one. He reminded him of a kind of ostrich—yes, that was probably the closest he could get to describing him. That description did a good job with his head, that beak of his, those beady, soulless eyes . . . though who really among the mythical creatures really had a soul? . . . and it at least went some way to explaining his neck too. The rest, though . . . *ah*, that was a different matter.

His torso was more of something approaching a brown, or maybe black bear, Q'oorth really couldn't have told the difference. He was *furry,* that was perhaps what he was trying to get at.

Thick fur, stick-your-hand-into-it-and-spread-out-your-fingers thick.

That sort of thick.

And he had a single leg. But five feet at the end of it, as if to compensate.

Yes, indeedy, Merv really was one *interesting* specimen.

And that visual went no way at all to describing the odour—
what Q'oorth had often heard as being likened to a mix between
sulphur pits and gnat wee . . . whatever either of those things
smelled of . . . or the jarring, stone-on-stone *scrape* of his joints,
which caused beasts from anywhere within the bar to crunch their
teeth together and hunch their shoulders.

Those with ears, in any case.

Currently, Merv stood off to one side behind the bar counter,
playing some sort of game out of sight that involved the flicking of
coins and the—very—occasional *tinkle* of said coins against the rim
of a glass. Not easily accomplished, either, considering that Merv
only had spiny, clawlike constructions to play with by way of hands.
Still, it sounded like more fun than, well, whatever Q'oorth was
doing here on this beaten-up old bar stool.

Q'oorth slugged back the flagon of brandy ale, listened to the
liquid splash all about his stony guts, heard it make a slightly acidic
hiss as it came into contact with his insides. He set the emptied
glass down on the counter with a wooden *thunk* which caused Merv
to snap his neck up to look over at him. Well, actually, his neck sort
of creaked dully, in the way that well-rusted church doors have a
habit of doing.

"'Nother?" Merv said, his voice a gut-wrenching, blood-curling
squawk.

. . . At least that was what Q'oorth had been told by those who
possessed blood and guts.

Q'oorth gave a stony nod.

Merv hopped his way along the bar, took Q'oorth's flagon with
those unlikely claw fingers of his—the ones that made Q'oorth
recall flaccid peacock feathers—and maneuvered the flagon below
the bar. As Merv uncorked a fresh, green bottle of brandy ale
using his beak, he slipped Q'oorth one of his expert barman's
looks. When he spat out the cork with a neat *kwack* sound, and

set about pouring the ale into the flagon, he casually sprung up conversation.

"Lookin' glum, my son."

That was another thing about Merv. He talked in rhymes. Something that, ordinarily, would've really got on Q'oorth's nerves after . . . well, the first couplet really . . . but given that Merv was such an 'interesting' specimen, he tolerated it.

Q'oorth gave him his best gargoyle's growl in response. It sounded a bit like a far-off thunderclap echoing through a deserted abbey.

"If there's anything on yer chest, getting' it out's the best."

Q'oorth looked Merv over. Just looking over him, Q'oorth knew that *he* had never had any problems not getting noticed. Merv had surely taken on this job here—in this bar, away from the Mortal realm—so that he *wouldn't* get noticed any longer.

"Ay? Anythin' to say?" Merv put in, as he recorked the bottle of brandy ale, and juggled it onto the ramshackle shelf behind him, somehow managing to get it back without it slipping through his claws and smashing at his feet.

Q'oorth breathed in then out again, only realising that his exhale sounded a lot like a sigh when he'd already gone and done it. When he looked up from his fresh flagon of brandy ale, he found Merv staring back at him, head slightly cocked to one side, in that understanding way beloved of barkeeper's throughout the Mortal and mythical realms.

"I . . . I . . ." Q'oorth began, somewhat unconvincingly, and then reminded himself who was the one made out of stone here. "I want to be *noticed*," he said.

"That so? How's it then, bro?"

Q'oorth gave the matter another second's thought and then decided that, really, he had nothing to lose from spilling his guts to the barkeep. Aside from anything else, he really had no guts to spill, *per se.* "Nowadays, in this modern age, everyone's got their own distractions, y'know? I thought it was bad, back last century, what with all those ghost stories. That was the start of it, I'm sure . . . the thing that started all that, that . . . *satire*," Q'oorth said it with real bile.

Merv stuck out his lower beak in a kind of pout and nodded along.

Q'oorth guessed, if his claws had allowed for it, that he'd be wiping down a glass right now. But cleanliness was probably the price paid for keeping a majority of glasses in one piece.

Like a pigeon with an upset tummy, Q'oorth kept on going. "Then this century, the seventies, the eighties, all those horror films —all that *terror* people got themselves exposed to. I thought *that* would be the end, that all the *wonder* had gone out of it, y'know?"

"Hmm," Merv said, but apparently could think of nothing to rhyme with it.

Q'oorth was grateful. "But, still, people were afraid—I saw it on their faces, in the graveyards, dodging through the place quickly, still a little terror." He tried his best to sigh again, and it came out quite successfully, all things considered. "But no, now I'm convinced that *this* is the end. Right here and now."

"Care to elaborate, 'fraid I might salivate?"

Q'oorth blinked a couple of times, trying to make sense of Merv. Sometimes he was certain that he just sprouted nonsense to stick with his rhyming *thing*.

Not that Q'oorth could complain.

At least Merv was *interesting*.

"Phones," Q'oorth said, finally, and the word might as well have been 'tombstones'. "That's the problem now, everyone, just *everyone*, all of them necks twisted down, looking over the screens. Not even got time to look up in terror at the gargoyles hanging down off the belfries, that's the gist of it."

Merv nodded sympathetically.

"I guess that's how it is, though. Things change, I know that, things become . . . *superfluous*."

For a long time there was a taut silence in the whole bar, and Q'oorth was sure that he'd just about spilled a little too much of his 'guts' . . . not that there was any taking it back now, and at least there wasn't really anybody else about the place to listen in, and laugh, about what he'd just said. Q'oorth was almost certain that Merv had given up on him, that he'd drifted off into his own thoughts—Merv *had* spent all eternity with mopey-headed, drunken mythical creatures.

That, Q'oorth speculated, was more likely the true definition of a 'hard shift'.

Finally, though, Merv did speak up. He leaned over the counter and dropped his voice, though there was no one about. "Here. This might not be your year, but you heard of this thing, real and true as your wings, call it winding back the bells, you know? . . . More curious do you grow?"

"Tell me more," Q'oorth said.

2

THOUGH SELF-LOATHING was an extremely strong term, Q'oorth had to admit that he had spent a good amount of time approximating at least something of it. Oh, sure, he was supposed to be *above* that, and there were some who might argue that he was *incapable* of that, but he knew the truth. He had seen the Mortals weaving about the graveyards, meandering in that way they did, eyes dipped down to the footpath they walked, hands in pockets, all *sorry* for themselves.

Well, Q'oorth had been that way for quite a time, even if *they* claimed that he didn't have the capacity to do so. He would show *them* all . . . though he knew that he would no doubt have quite a hard time in proving the mostly indifferent fate, time, space—or whatever else it was supposed to be called—wrong in the long run.

But, godsdammit, he'd give it something of a shot!

Because now he had the answer. If Merv wasn't playing some elaborate practical joke on him, he was sure that he had the answer.

So he got himself back to his haunt, went through all the palaver of swilling about through the various parallel realities and ended up on Evermoore Church, in his familiar position in the belfry.

Everything looked pretty much as it had done before, all things considered. The battered, old bells still hung there all covered in cobwebs and smelling musty. His companions, or his *Eternal Companions*, as he was supposed to term them: Fing'um, Yort'hard and Chork remained in their frozen positions, eyes glowering, teeth bared, claws all spread out.

These were the aforementioned *conservative* friends.

The ones that *feigned* indifference to being invisible to the people down below—to *not* being really frightening at all, while they each had their own little vain rituals . . .

Why, Q'oorth couldn't think of a single pigeon that had so much as dared lift its haunches that had got off this belfry with its life. Although it had been more than a decade since the last fundraiser that'd seen cleaners rising up here, to the belfry, giving everything a touch of warm water and soap, there wasn't one spot of guano to be spied.

Q'oorth looked to his perch, its splash of cement where they'd 're-glued' him about fifty years ago following a particularly nasty storm. His perch faced east . . . toward the church gates.

His was the box seat.

His was *supposedly* the most cherished spot of any gargoyle in this churchyard.

He had, once or twice, noticed another of his companions making eyes at his position, obviously intently interested in maybe seeing just how they might suit the role.

. . . They had something of reason, too. Not since the advent of these *damn* phones had Q'oorth been able to send a half satisfying twitch of terror down a Mortal's spine.

That would all change, though.

Right now.

Rather than venturing to his mark, he headed inside the belfry, taking care not to bump his head on the wooden shutters. He took in the bells.

All of them hung from their battered beam.

Six in all.

Q'oorth thought back to the advice he'd got from Merv. Then set about putting it into practice.

Turn each bell around one full cycle on its rafter.

Up and over.

So simple.

It *had* to be a joke.

When Q'oorth glanced over his shoulder, he noticed that his companions were looking at him funny. That they were all giving him that flat, slightly hangdog-like stare . . .

Finally, he got through the entire row. Having wound each bell back, he sat on his haunches and waited. When he looked to his companions, he saw that two of them were now looking at him, while another—Chork—was eyeing up Q'oorth's vacant position.

No doubt he was thinking very strongly about taking it up . . . but, before he could make a move of any kind, the world began to spin. To whirl about before his eyes. He saw colours—*so many colours!*

And, for some reason, it was only then that he really thought about the seriousness of what he had done. Ah well, too late now . . .

3

I T WAS THE SMELL, more than anything, that let Q'oorth know he'd been successful. It was . . . and, really, there's no polite way of saying it . . . the stench of human crap.

And horse crap.

And pig crap.

And cow crap.

And a whole multitude of crap that probably extended the whole web of the animal kingdom.

Hell, there was probably even some dormouse crap mixed in there somewhere too.

Not that it bothered Q'oorth all that much. That was one of the benefits of having stone nostrils. Along with the benefit of having a stone stomach. He didn't need metaphors since he had the real thing. He was stone, through and through.

He looked to his companions, to Fing'um, Yort'hard and Chork.

They were, all of them, blinking dimwittedly at him. Obviously unable to quite believe just what had happened. He guessed that, when he'd wound back the bells, they'd come along with him for the ride. Fair enough, all things considered.

He also noted that Chork, once again, was eyeing up his spot. It was a shame that, for what Q'oorth had in mind, he wouldn't be able to step between dimensions, freeze time like when he went to Merv's bar so that he could ensure that none of his 'companions' had the opportunity to steal his spot while he was gone. But, if he could just get done what he had in mind, then it really wouldn't matter *who* took up the spot which faced the gates to the graveyard.

He beat his wings. Once, twice. A few more times.

Just for effect really, since stone wings, at least in the Mortal realm, really did very little for aerodynamics.

He looked about him, figured the best way down was—uncontroversially—the spiral steps which ran down the centre of the bell tower. He flashed Chork what he thought was a menacing glare of warning, and then he set off, headed right down the steps, till he got to ground level.

The churchyard today was totally deserted, and he had the opportunity to scope out the surrounding area. All the modern buildings that had surrounded the graveyard for the best part of the last century had gone. In fact, there were no buildings at all. Just mulchy-green and brown fields surrounding on all sides. Yes, stretching his mind back now, he *could* remember.

He remembered how things had been back here and now—somewhere about the turn of the first millennium.

He loped his way off along the muddy path, toward the graveyard gate.

Before he slipped out, down onto the rock-strewn path which had replaced the tarmac road of a few minutes before, he flashed a glance upward, to the belfry.

Chork had taken his chance, at last. He had gone and taken his perch.

That was fine, though . . . at least that was what Q'oorth told himself as he slipped out through the rickety wooden gate and loped his way off down the stony-walled lane, and in the direction of the little village.

4

ALL THINGS CONSIDERED, Q'oorth had expected to run into more humans, but he was surprised to find that—on the contrary—there really weren't that many humans about.

Were they indoors?

Working the fields?

Off to market for the day?

Q'oorth really had no idea. He'd got so used to seeing humans about *everywhere* that he had forgotten that there had been a time when humans had been a relatively sparse feature. He was still wondering whether or not this was a good or bad thing, when, up ahead, he spotted a child: a boy, no more than eight or nine years old, kicking a rock across the road.

The boy wore rags, that same mulchy-brown as the fields, and Q'oorth speculated that, most likely, he had the same mulchy-green colour sprouting all over his teeth, too.

If there's one thing gargoyles can't abide by, it's letting mould and other things spring up all over the place, at their own whim.

This was it.

Just as he'd planned it.

He just had to . . .

Before he could think through his approach anymore, the boy spotted him, his eyes rolled upward, and his mouth latched open, kind of like a tamed, and lazy, snake waiting for its owner to place its breakfast between its jaws. The boy didn't really do anything more. It was almost like he was waiting for permission to scream, and Q'oorth, being a fairly benevolent creature as he was, most likely would've given it to him if he'd asked . . . and on any *other* day, he might not have minded. But today he had a real use for him.

Q'oorth loped closer, gradually closing the gap between the two of them. Before he knew it, they were nose to nose. All told, they were just about the same height . . . not much more than four feet or so. "Uh, hello?" Q'oorth said.

The boy just continued to eyeball him.

"Your parents about?"

The boy's features remained frozen.

"Ah . . . nobody else about town today, then?"

No response.

Q'oorth subtly looked past the boy, trying to see if there might be a better prospect about town, someone who was a mite more skilled in conversation. Not seeing anybody, he tried the boy again. "Uh, Mummy? Daddy?"

This time the boy did react, albeit very subtly. His bottom lip began to wobble and his eyes started to water. A very slight, almost inaudible, whine of fear came from his throat.

Again, on another day, perhaps the very response Q'oorth would have expected.

Not really what he needed now, though.

Ah, well, maybe it was better to make the best he could out of a bad bundle.

Q'oorth decided to get going on his plan. "What I need, uh, from you . . . *Mortal*," he added after much consternation, and from that slight unease at hearing his stony voice in the presence of a human. "Well, this . . . this is going to be just a little tricky to explain, so bear with me, please. Basically, uh, aside from being a walking, talking gargoyle, I come from the future, uh, do you understand that?"

The boy remained just as wide eyed as before, and similarly on the verge of tears.

"Look, it's all very well back here, you now in . . . uh, what year is it exactly?"

No reply.

Unsurprisingly.

"Fine," Q'oorth said, determined to get through this. "My problem—and let me lay this out as clearly as I can—my *problem* is people are simply not afraid of mythical statues any longer, yes?"

The boy said nothing to confirm he had heard, let alone understood this.

"I can even, uh, do just what I'm doing now. You know, go walking about them, and people just pat me on the head and laugh, and that's at best, see? They think that I'm someone all dressed up . . ." Q'oorth thought that one through a little better, reminded himself that he'd passed through a thousand years and no doubt needed to gauge his language somewhat ". . . uh, they don't believe that I'm a mythical beast at all, you see? They just think that I'm another Mortal, like you?"

Q'oorth reminded himself that it was never convincing in an argument to raise intonation at the end of a sentence, to make a question of something which was a perfectly serviceable statement. He trusted that this wasn't on the forefront of the boy's mind, and decided that it was best for him to hedge his bets. He thought back to himself, remembering how Merv had claimed that for each turn of the bells he would be given one hour in the past.

One hour to make the changes he required.

"So," he said, "basically what I need you to do is, well, sort of tell people about me, you know? Tell them that they've got to be afraid—no, *extremely* afraid of all things gargoyle."

He thought about the others: the dragons, the griffins and—worst of all—the unicorns . . . why, they'd been given a real namby-pamby write-up over the years, and not a morning passed without Q'oorth giving his thanks that he'd not been brought into being as a unicorn . . . then again, if he didn't get this thing done right now, gargoyles might go exactly the same way . . . and that didn't bear thinking about.

"So . . ." he said, "what're you going to tell . . ."

But now he saw the boy was looking beyond him, off over his stone wings, off down the pathway that led out of town, and toward the church.

Q'oorth guesstimated that he had about ten minutes, at best, left here.

Better to get a hurry on, get this boy to agree to what it was he wanted him to do, make sure that the plan of action was solid in his feeble Mortal mind.

All the same, Q'oorth did follow his eyes, did look back over his shoulder.

Ah, that was where the villagers had got to!

The dozen or so of them—no doubt all cousins, and other very close relations.

They all had that same look of complete and total shock on their faces.

The same expression as the boy.

This would be *far* more effective.

He was on the brink of addressing them right when the first woman shrieked. One of those 'blood-curdling' shrieks he had heard so much about!

And then—just like that, all of a sudden—people were dashing about, running into their houses, locking up their doors.

Q'oorth looked to where the boy had been.

He was gone.

Been whipped away by his eagle-eyed mother, no doubt.

He supposed he would just have to trust that he'd done enough here since time was running out.

He had to be getting back to the belfry.

THE TRANSITION BACK to the present was much like going back into the past. This time, though, Q'oorth did it with a dirty great grin spread all over his stone face.

He thought about how he and his companions had just trod water—really, never got themselves down there, at ground level, getting their hands dirty, and how it had come back to bite them.

Sometimes people truly needed to *see* something for it to have a proper impact.

Even across centuries.

. . . At least that had been his brainwave.

So, back up on the belfry, he looked down on the second millennium—*century number twenty-one*. He surveyed the churchyard.

It was much as it had been before. Not a human in sight.

Not yet.

But he could wait.

He had to take up Chork's perch since Chork had stolen his own. Q'oorth was sure that Chork felt a long way from comfortable. He'd know all too well that the other two would be actively plotting his downfall . . . and that Q'oorth himself would be looking to regain his lost ground.

Patience, for a gargoyle, was really the very epitome of the craft. To be fair, there's a lot of standing-slash-crouching to be done.

All things considered, he had it pretty nice compared to other gargoyles he'd seen on his travels, the ones that had only a narrow ledge above a drainpipe, or who had to kneel up on buttresses, that sort of thing. No, Q'oorth wouldn't trade his belfry for the world, even if he was now facing off to the south, rather than his rightful place facing to the east.

Soon enough, the first Mortal wandered along. Phone clutched in hand, staring down at the screen, it headed up the graveyard path, no doubt on its way to paying its respects . . . thoroughly *ignoring* all aspects of the church itself—Q'oorth, and the gargoyles, were no exception to that.

Q'oorth waited. Felt the light breeze whistle past his stone ears, beat about his stone horns.

Patience.

It's all about . . .

Right then, just as the Mortal was about to turn around the side of the church, it jerked its head upward. And Q'oorth saw its mouth open wide, its eyes loll back in their sockets, and a *true* expression of terror pass over its floppy little face.

The same look of fear that boy, a thousand years back, had shown him.

That right there—down there—looking up at him, was the definition of success.

Q'oorth watched on with great smugness, as the Mortal pocketed its phone, then, with another few cursory glances upward to Q'oorth and his companions, wound its way around the side of the church. Only when the Mortal was out of sight did Q'oorth catch Chork's eye.

They exchanged a long stare which said many things, but above all it said, 'Gerrof my perch!' and that was just what Chork did, because Q'oorth had done them all a service.

All the gargoyles of Evermoore Church.

And though they all stood hunched with their backs to one another, he could feel their looks of pride as they thought about their rightful leader:

Q'oorth.

The funny thing was, though, that his thinking didn't stop there.

In fact, he found himself stretching his mind to encompass

other gargoyles—all about the land, in other churches, all of them going ignored . . .

He wondered just what a little playing back in the past might do for them . . . might *fix* for them.

Because one thing was for sure, it was one of the mythical creatures' responsibilities to the world to never let that sense of wonder ever fully get away.

Never to let it escape Mortal minds completely.

And now Q'oorth had the tool—the tool to make the world right again.

He could wind back bells.

ESCAPE THE MOUNTAIN!!

ASH PUMPED OUT from the crater of the volcano, blackening the air.

Carol Matthews felt her lungs prickle with the thick smoke and the sheer heat. She tried to hold her breath. The ash rocketed from the crater with a noise that reminded her of the freight trains which would shoot past the bottom of her garden back at her childhood home.

She couldn't hold her breath any longer and let out a quick exhale, before a rapid breath inward.

She tasted the ash in her mouth—up her nostrils.

She stumbled and felt herself back into something solid.

Pain flashed from the base of her spine.

The rock face.

Without needing to look around she knew that the drop was thousands of feet. The only alternative was for her to move forward, to step into the thick, searing-hot smoke gushing from the crater. The heat was almost too much to bear now, it slicked up her back, sent the sweat slipping down her spine. Soaking through her undershirt and going through her zip-up fleece—the one that'd seemed necessary just that morning, as she'd woken up in her tent, peered out through the flap and seen the fog rolling down the foothills.

As she felt her heart rapping at her throat, she thought about how she'd got herself into this mess all because she'd got lost and hadn't wanted to ask for help.

Those walkers, back up the path, they might've been able to tell her how to get down to the village safely. But she hadn't wanted to bother them. She'd been too polite.

And now it might get her killed.

She pressed herself flat against the rock, trying to feel for something—*anything*—that might provide hope of escape. A chance of getting out alive.

She refused to take her eyes off the crater, as if it represented the jaws of a rabid dog—as if it was just as wild and unpredictable . . . actually, thinking about it, it was probably *far* more unpredictable than a rabid dog, what with the volcano being thoroughly indifferent to a living, breathing . . . sweating . . . specimen.

Just as she felt the heat grow to be too much to bear—felt like her skin might melt clean off her bones—her fingers ran over something plastic . . . yes, it was plastic—wasn't it?

. . . Or, no, plastic surely would've melted long ago up here. But then it would've had to be metal. And metal—as she well knew from the science lessons engrained in her mind ever since school—got hotter when introduced to heat.

But this *thing* wasn't hot at all . . . and, if she just—*yes!*—shoved down hard on it, she felt it give way, and felt herself falling backward.

Falling and falling.

Tumbling head over heel.

Dropping down into obsidian gloom.

She had time to think. Time to *cool* off.

She wondered how long she would keep falling—if she'd simply go on forever.

Or if she'd—

Something soft and springy broke her fall.

When she hit, she felt herself sinking into the material. It reminded her of a trampoline. It seemed to suck up all the energy she'd accumulated as part of her fall.

And then—all of a sudden—she was thrust back upward.

Back up in the direction where she had fallen down.

Toward the volcano once more.

Her gut churned.

Only a second or so later did she realise she was descending again.

Headed back down for that trampoline . . . or whatever it was.

She managed a good few snappy breaths, just about managing to get her brain back on functioning terms. She hit the flexible material once more.

Bounced again, though this time not so high.

She repeated this process till she reached a well-earned standstill.

She lay for a long moment, just taking in her surroundings, trying to get her heartrate back under *some* sort of control.

She breathed out that ashy smoke, and breathed in the—*slightly manky, stilted and sulphur-edged, but otherwise fine*—air.

It was pleasantly warm, and she wondered whether she'd dropped down a fair way . . . close enough to get the warmth from the core of the earth, in any case.

But that was ridiculous thinking.

Then again, she couldn't really say for certain. She had no particular science—or had it been geography?—recollection to illuminate this one.

All told, it was a tad tricky to see anything. Which was to say, actually, that it was completely and totally *pitch* black. She wondered whether she'd ever seen a blackness this black before. She hadn't reached any meaningful conclusion by the time she heard that shallow, fairly long-off-sounding cackle.

She jerked her head to look.

And was disappointed.

She felt about, felt the trampoline-like material beneath her and, slowly, lifted herself up into something resembling a sitting position using her elbows for crutches.

"Hello?" she said.

The cackle seemed to grow so that it echoed all about her, and then, all of a sudden, it simply dropped off altogether, slipped back off into silence.

She regretted having said anything at all since silence was much worse than at least hearing *something* out there in the obscurity. Whereas before she'd felt afraid, now she felt alone *and* afraid. She decided to give it another go, another, "Hello?" but the only response to her call was her own words again bouncing off the —*rock?*—walls.

She lay where she was. Not wanting to move a muscle lest she find herself crawling into a lava pit, or whatever it was that they kept down in very dark holes near to the centre of the earth. This trampoline-like thing had served her well so far, saved her from certain death, no less, so there seemed no sense in leaving what she knew so well . . . leaving what she knew had almost got her killed just today, up there on that ledge, overlooking that volcano.

Just thinking about it sent a warm flush through her cheeks. She reached up and felt her face—felt her cheeks having returned to, all things considered, a fairly normal temperature.

Neither dripping with sweat nor flaking off till all she had was bone.

That was a plus.

The only real negatives about all this were that: one, she didn't have a rope to get out of this place—though, admittedly, it was fairly doubtful there was enough rope in the world to compensate for the distance she'd just fallen—and, two, that there was someone who seemed to enjoy cackling, scaring people who'd just recently dropped down onto this well-place trampoline-like thing.

She just sat-slash-lay there, elbows propping her up, shoulders arched back, and stared upward—*up?*—into the obscurity that pressed down on her head.

She could see nothing, of course, but it did make her feel

marginally better to consider that up there—*somewhere*—beyond the mounted-up earth, and mud, and rock, and whatever, the sun was still beaming down on the world.

Wasn't it?

Or was this some sort of—

"Awright there?"

Carol startled. She gazed off in the direction of the greeting. Made no inroads into guessing just precisely where it'd come from.

"I *said*, 'Awright there?' "

Again, she couldn't put an accurate direction on just where those words had come from. She spun herself about, as if whoever —whatever?—this was it might glow in the dark.

As it happened, she was in luck. Because this particular *thing* . . . and it *was* a thing as it turned out . . . *did* glow in the dark.

A light purple, shimmering glow, one that made her think back of Christmas lights on the high street of her home town: the ones that made her wonder why the local authorities had never actually plumped for red and green lights, being more traditionally 'Christmas' as they were, but then again the local authorities had always been cheap, and there was the argument to be made for multiculturalism, given that Carol could hear a half dozen different languages just walking to the shops, and that those people of other cultures paid their taxes just like the rest, and of course it made sense not to go out of the way to offend . . .

"Heeellllloooowww?" the luminous *thing* said.

Carol blinked herself back to the present. Took in its form for the first time, saw that it had little, goat-like horns, and a bulging belly with leathered skin, and downy black hair covering parts that, she supposed, would have been gratuitous if they'd been on show.

She felt a lump form in her throat, but was determined that—this time—she was going to make the effort to use her words, you know, those things she'd learned about and used every day back in that aforementioned *school* of hers.

The thing stood upright, on top of the trampoline-like surface that she lay-slash-sat on, and it was about ten or fifteen paces away from her, though it could've been further away considering that her perception was a little screwy due to the poor lighting.

"Are you . . . are you . . . ?"

"What?" the thing said, grinning, showing off rows and rows of spiky teeth.

They were just about the same tone as his skin, which was *sallow* to say the least.

The whole aspect of the thing kind of suggested 'jaundice' to Carol.

. . . But, no—*no labels!*—hadn't her psychiatrist gone on about that with her, told her that she had to *stop* doing that, packing people down into easily biteable chunks so she wouldn't have to deal with the rag-a-tag, stitched-together, and wondrous, blanket of humanity.

"Go on," the thing said, sounding a touch excitable, "I wuv to hear the things you humans have to say."

"Us . . . us . . ."

The thing—he-slash-she-slash-it—made a kind of circular motion with their finger, signalling for her to go on.

"Uh, a . . . a *devil?*" she got out finally.

The thing's smile dimmed just a little and it seemed like the jaundice-yellow glow left its eyes. "Ah," it said, "Yes, that's a popuwlar one—was hoping for more originawl, but there you go, can't have surprises every day, otherwise they wouldn't be surprises, would they?"

"Uh, I suppose not."

"Naw," the thing said, now sounding, and looking, totally dejected.

Carol wondered offhand if he—perhaps—might have some sort of a self-esteem issue, but it wasn't her prerogative to pry into the lives of others . . . that was another lesson from her psychiatrist, and one that'd served her pretty well too; kept her from social exclusion and all that sort of stuff that she had previously labelled as bad but learned—with the aid of her psychiatrist—was just undesirable.

The thing, she noticed now, as her eyes grew more accustomed to the odd, light-purple light, carried an odd, hobbly, knobbly staff with him. It had several notches in it, and it curled up to the top with a smooth, wavelike wooden carving. She guessed that the thing—or whoever had created the staff—had spent a fair amount of time on it. Most likely there wasn't all that much going on down here, in the depths of the underground, so probably a good place to practise craft skills.

The thing seemed to be scratching away at something on the trampoline-like surface with the butt of its staff. She could feel the slight vibrations passing beneath her.

For some reason she felt a great need to bring up his spirits, despite the fact that he was clearly at home down here, and she clearly was not. In short, she was the one in need, and this thing was very much in good hands, as far as fate was concerned.

"Uh, would you like to hear a joke?" Carol asked.

The thing stopped its scratching, extended her the courtesy of tilting its head upward and looking at her. "No one's towld me a joke before."

"No?"

The thing shook its head, extremely dolefully.

Carol searched her brains. Just like always, she'd spoken before thinking things through completely. That was another one of her 'hang-ups', another thing which—with the good hand of Doctor Lleelup . . . her psychiatrist—she had hoped to nip in the bud.

She scrambled up, finding the ground beneath her strangely solid—not at all like the trampoline-like surface from before, much more like concrete now.

"Uh," she started, somewhat unconvincingly, and remembered . . . . this time not something her psychiatrist had instructed her, but a former boyfriend . . . how un*lady*like it sounded for her to begin every sentence with 'uh'.

But sometimes she couldn't help it.

"Uh," she said again, then, "There were once these, uh, two people in this, uh, kitchen . . . no, wait, I've, uh, said that wrong." She watched as the thing's expression warped from one of extreme expectation into one of imminent disappointment. "Uh, and then . . ."

"No," the thing said, holding up its hand-slash-claw . . . "Reawlly, don't worry about it . . ."

"No, I think I can . . ."

The thing shook its head with finality. "A nice thought—a really nice thought—and I'm sure it would've cheered me up, but I have things I need to do." The thing heaved its horny shoulders, gave a stomach-deep sigh, then added, "Work, work, work, eh?"

Carol noted a slight smile on the thing's lips, and did her best to smile back. She felt a tiny warm glow at the pit of her lungs.

"Right," the thing said, its tone hardening a little, "Here's the wowdown."

She guessed he meant 'lowdown'.

The way the thing spoke it seemed like he'd picked up expressions and phrases from films, or from music, or something . . . but not from regular, everyday conversations. He had the air of someone who'd learned English from tapes, got all the basics, all the grammar down, but just hadn't quite had the opportunity to practise and put all those bits and pieces of theory together into fluency. And that odd speech impediment didn't make things any easier.

Was that how Doctor Lleelup would have phrased it—or was there some more politically correct way of saying it? 'Speech imped-iment' sounded fairly clinical to her—admittedly—tin ear.

"I am what is known as a Game Keeper."

"A what?" Carol said, again a little lost in her own thoughts.

. . . Yet another thing Doctor Lleelup was on the back of his noble, silver-haired steed trying to cure.

The thing cleared its throat, or appeared to . . . it made all the appropriate sounds, whatever the case. "A Game Keeper."

"Oh, and what's that?"

The thing blinked a couple of times. Calloused, crusty eyelids that seemed to have greeny, sludge-textured mucus permanently smeared onto them.

"Sorry," she said, "Is it obvious? Is it something that's—you know—just totally palm-to-forehead stupid?"

The thing cocked its head to one side and pouted.

Maybe she had to make a better job of explaining herself.

"You see," she said, "I've just come through, well, I suppose it'd be what you'd call 'an episode'"—she actually made the quotation marks with her fingers—"and, well, I've been taking time away, getting my feet back on the ground, spending more time outdoors and until today . . . until the *volcano*, I thought I was doing rather well." She paused a moment, remembering again, another piece of advice from her psychiatrist—think about the other person in the conversation, give them time to digest, to *hear* what you're saying, before moving onto the next thing. "And then, well. I got caught up there, stuck by the volcano, and then fell all the way down here."

The thing closed one eye as if sizing her up.

"Am I dead?" she asked, feeling a little exasperated.

The thing shook its head.

"Ah, that's okay then."

"You're in limbo."

Carol felt like her brain was weighing down her spine. But she stayed standing. Kept herself still. Practised her breathing exercises and—just like Doctor Lleelup always suggested—waited to feel the blood trickling slowly through her veins, her heart pounding just a little more gently.

She looked the thing . . . the Game Keeper . . . up and down, then said, "So, am I alive?"

The Game Keeper shook his head.

"Ah."

The Game Keeper inspected his staff in a bored sort of a way, as if checking to see if there was any angle that he might go about sanding down later when he wasn't on the job. She could tell he took pride in his appearance—the crusty weirdness on his eyelids aside, of course.

"So, uh, what's coming up next?" she asked.

The Game Keeper, still keeping his eye fixed to his staff spoke in a lower voice, as if he was a prompter working an amateur production, helping the leading lady out with a few cues, to get her back on course with her lines. "Aren't you going to ask about my name?"

"Your name?"

"Yes."

"But, your name, is it . . . uh . . ."

"The Game Keeper."

"That's a title, not a *name*."

The Game Keeper gave another of those sighs, thought it sufficient to flex an eye in Carol's general direction, and then said, "Title, name, it's all the same down here."

"Oh, I see," she said, though she really didn't. "What does your title . . . *name* mean?"

Another of those sighs, and then the thing said, "As Game Keeper it is my duty to inform you that you have used one of the Ways Out in your world, and come tumbling down into this one which sits . . ." he eyed Carol rather thoroughly, in the same way that Doctor Lleelup did sometimes, when he was lowering the register of his explanations to her level . . . maybe Carol should've been insulted but, to be honest, she was used to it ". . . kind of in the space between the Now, and the Then, the Before and the After, if that makes sense?"

"Oh yes," Carol said with a nod, knowing that it didn't.

The Game Keeper slipped her a wry, and slightly arrogant smile. "Fine, that's just fine—the upshot of this whole deawl is that you're no wonger what we would construe as human, and . . ."

Carol held up her hand. "Wait, wait," she said, "What was that thing you said about Ways Out?"

" 'Ways Out' ?"

"Yes?"

The Game Keeper gave a smirk that suggested he was going a little beyond his duty in explaining this thing, and that he would've rather have got done with his business, all told, about ten or fifteen minutes ago, and be off doing . . . oh, whatever it was Game Keepers did . . .

"A Way Out," the Game Keeper explained, "comes about whenever a person is in mortawl periwl, that is, on the cusp of losing their life . . . just as you were up there by that vowlcano?" He eyed her. "We understand one another?"

She nodded, maybe a little too vigorously, but she was keen to ram home the point that she *did* follow him.

"You shouwld reawlly be congratuwlated, because, bewlieve me, it is not every human that manages to come across a Way Out."

"So why *aren't* you congratulating me?"

"Because it's not reawlly something to be congratuwlated—I mean, where you've ended up, down here with me."

"So what happens now?"

"You have a choice to make."

She tried to keep herself together, though she could certainly feel the beginnings of her mind beginning to unwind, all that meticulous psychological conditioning that Doctor Lleelup had put her through was being ruined. All told, she didn't supposed he'd designed the treatment to stand up under conditions such as this one, stepping a little outside of the mortal realm. But she was determined that she had the tools to see herself through this thing and come out the other side of it smelling of roses.

She looked the Game Keeper over. He was rolling his shoulders and neck, apparently trying to loosen tension. "So, you're saying this is all some sort of a—*I dunno* . . . game?"

When she caught the Game Keeper's eye she had never before seen someone trying so hard to restrain themselves from giving a slow handclap.

That would've been *terrible* for her self-esteem.

"And, uh, it's up to me whether or not I go back?"

The Game Keeper nodded.

"And what're the conditions of it, then?"

"If you choose to go back, you shall be returned to the instant of another's position of peril, put into someone else's shoes, a person who also chose to take a Way Out . . . though whether or not they chose to go to the Hereafter or spin the wheel again is up to them . . . upon arriving in another's body you will be required to overcome said peril, and—"

"What if I get killed?"

"Killed?" the Game Keeper replied, and then smiled—the first smile in the whole meeting that seemed truly genuine and deep felt. "You'll die," he added finally, with great satisfaction.

"I see."

"What's it to be then, spin the wheel, or wander on off in the Afterlife?"

"I, uh . . ."

"I'm sorry, that's a tricky question, I shouldn't put it so bluntly."

"What's, uh, beyond there, in the Afterlife, I mean?"

The Game Keeper puffed out his cheeks and raised his eyebrows. "Oh, nothing much really. You like floating, don't you? Bright-white lights? Twenty-four-hour harp music, that sort of thing?"

Carol thought about it for a moment. "Not really."

The Game Keeper shrugged. "Can't say that you'd get much of a kick out of the Afterlife, then."

She thought this over hard. Thought about her life. The way the Game Keeper laid all these things out, the way that he put it, she would leave her body behind here . . . or someone else would take possession of it . . . but what about—and then she realised that she had the expert at hand right here, so not much point in speculating.

"Do I, you know—?"

"Keep your memories," the Game Keeper interjected, smugly, "your personality, that sort of thing?"

She nodded.

"Yes, of course, everything that's packaged with your soul."

"Soul?"

The Game Keeper waved it away, as if he regretted ever bringing it up. "So, come on, time to choose. Time's a wasting . . . well, not here, not really . . . but I've got better things to do than stand around marking out eternity, you know?"

She gave it a little more thought—thought about how she'd

spent so much time with Doctor Lleelup trying to stitch up her fraught mind, and that would all have been in vain, just to go about floating in bright whiteness, listening to harp music . . .

No, she was determined. She'd always been a fighter. She wouldn't throw it all away.

She wouldn't throw her life away over a touch of apprehension.

She looked the Game Keeper flush in those gleaming, diamond-like eyes of his and said, "Okay, I'll take another go at it."

The Game Keeper smiled thickly. "Glad to hear it," he said, and then jabbed his staff down hard on the floor a couple of times, making it give a pair of stiff *clicks*.

The whole world swirled about her, and she got the feeling of having a wave wash over her, before being dragged back in the undertow. The currents pulled her in all directions. And then she felt herself wet all over. Felt herself trembling.

She was in a bathtub.

In a house. *Somewhere.*

A bathroom, to be more specific.

Outside she saw there was a storm raging. In the near distance she could hear a rumble of thunder. Hail stones tinkled down onto the roof tiles.

Right away, she saw the issue. Saw the mortal peril which awaited her. It was a toaster. In her hands, and plugged into one of the wall sockets. It felt warm, and she saw that the grill within was glowing a fiery red. She was on the brink of laying the toaster down —*well* outside the bath—before a thought struck her.

She glanced about, looked to the peach-coloured tiles which ran up the wall to her right. Keeping the toaster very tight in one hand, she reached out and moved her hand along the tiles.

And she found it.

That plastic . . . steel? . . . whatever it was, it was a firm-feeling thing.

A *Way Out*.

This was interesting—very interesting *indeed*.

For a second, her hand rested against it and she thought about pulling it down.

What would happen then?

Would she reset, go back to see the Game Keeper, get another chance at choosing another body?

Another life?

. . . In the end, the thing which swung it for her was looking down along her soaked body. She noticed the legs crawling with black hair—hundreds of spiders sleeping on her skin.

Moving her gaze up a little further, she got the firm proof she needed.

Yup, she was definitely a man.

This could be *interesting*.

One change to start off with.

She looked to the Way Out again, thought another time about what she'd discovered, and then set the toaster down on the floor, outside the bathtub. She ran her hand up along the tiled wall again, but couldn't feel anything.

The Way Out was gone.

As she got herself up and out of the tepid water, she reached for the fluffy white towel which hung down from a peg on the wall. Fairly novel that the previous owner of this body had had enough forethought—even while on the brink of suicide—to leave himself a towel to get dry if he changed his mind . . . then again, the man had had enough pause for thought to think to run his hand along the tiles to find the Way Out.

Or had he known about the Way Out all along?

Was that why he'd brought himself into this situation, put himself in a position of self-inflicted mortal peril?

She wrapped herself in the towel, tied it around her waist in a way that she'd often observed but never done herself, and then heard, off in the distance of the house, a female voice.

Shrill and uneven. A voice which turned her gut just a little.

And Carol gave a smirk thinking about the fun she was going to have in this new body.

DUENDE

FIVE HUNDRED YEARS AGO, I hitched a ride in a Spaniard's backpack. He was searching for El Dorado and I was looking fresh human souls. When the Spaniards were bent over, retching from hunger, I hopped off and ran into the Amazonian jungle.

I built my shack in five days. Twigs ran up the sides, set in place with hardened mud, while I made the roof from huge leaves—some the size of half-a-dozen human heads. I replaced them twice a year, or whenever I woke up with rain water dripping on my forehead.

Inside, hundreds of human souls in bottles were gathered along shelves, while others lay scattered under the bed. A green-white-soul glow illuminated my shack day and night. I was stitching a sail to carry me to the duende afterlife, which required a thousand souls.

The years passed by and the modern age rolled in. Over time, the natives were kind to me. Pure believers. Their souls were easy to steal and glowed brightest in the bottles. Key stones in my soul sail alongside their European cousins. Soon I had nine-hundred and ninety-nine.

Only one stood between me and salvation.

Nature seemed to urge me on too. Outside my shack, in the distance, axes bit and chainsaws snarled. Time was running out. Mankind was eating its way into the last of the world's great unknown—kicking out the supernatural and replacing it with reason and civilisation. Every day they came closer to discovering me.

It was time to fill the last bottle.

RAIN LASHED DOWN and the air smelled salty, reminding me of the long voyage across the Atlantic, the days and months hidden inside a barrel of sea biscuits. I skittered over wet ground, shuddering when I stepped over my zone of influence—marked in a thick white hex, visible only to duendes. Outside my influence, I could not cast spells affecting others. I had to find creative ways to catch souls in a nearby village.

Approaching the village, I hid behind a thick tree trunk. In the late-afternoon light, the sleepy village snoozed away—completely unaware how close danger lurked. A few people drifted about, not paying attention to the small details, broken twigs and rustling branches; leaving themselves open to attack.

I spied a young woman, all alone. I assumed she was fifteen or sixteen, considering her developed bust, but still girlish face. Her heart beat in my ears. I reached for her, but, like a cold wave, fear hit me and I retracted my claw.

The thought of the wise man crossed my mind. I'd had a few close brushes in the past, and didn't fancy another one. He had the power to send me straight to hell.

She raised her head, gasped and trotted away. Something had warned her. Perhaps my scent.

Lucky.

I hopped about the village, remaining hidden behind trunks, when I spotted another. It was a boy, perhaps ten years old.

Bare-chested, he crouched, skimming his fingers along the ground—no doubt torturing some hapless insect. Nature screamed out in pain, pleading for my help.

After a quick glance around, I muttered an incantation. My stubby arms and legs sprouted great, hairy human skin and my legs grew out of my ankles. I took a deep breath and emerged from my hiding place, in the exact appearance of the boy's uncle.

I stood and waved.

A flicker passed across his eyes and I thought he would scream out—call on the wise man to dispose of me. My heart raced, but I retained my easy smile. I needed the last soul.

He stood up and approached me on sleepy feet. "Uncle?"

I stepped back into the jungle—willing him to follow. Over his head, I studied the village. There was no one else around. We were going to slip away.

About a hundred yards in, the boy hesitated. He looked around.

I gritted my teeth and trod on, trusting he would follow. After another moment's thought, he jogged to catch up.

We had walked on for a while, when I noticed the boy sizing up the trees. I grinned to reassure him. He was mine now, lost to the forest forever. Such a simple trick.

My mind already on the bottles, I realised the sound of footsteps had ceased. I spun round. Standing square on, the boy gazed into my face.

I kept up the same toothy grin, determined not to falter. Soon, we would reach my shack.

"You're not my uncle, are you?" he said.

I peeled back my lips, accentuating my smile.

"Why don't you speak?"

I trusted the boy would never find his way back. What choice did he have but to follow?

He strutted up and jabbed me in the stomach. "Take me back!"

Pulse thudding in my temples, I turned and ran. Branches scratched my arms and leaves crackled under my feet. I saw my shack up ahead.

Over my shoulder, the boy chased. He'd run straight into my trap.

I sprinted back into my zone of influence and skidded to a halt.

Panting, the boy trudged into the clearing. He stopped and ran his eyes up and down. "I know what you are, *duende*!"

His feet were inches from my influence.

If only he took another step, he would be mine.

He laughed, but he had white terror in his eyes. "I know where you live. I'll bring back the wise man and he'll send you to hell."

Dusk was rolling in.

I cleared my throat and said, "Boy?"

Paralysed in terror, his eyes widened.

"Congratulations. You've found me. It's getting dark. Why not spend the night with me. You can set out for the village tomorrow morning."

He stayed perfectly still.

Nerves jangling, my patience waned. I licked my lips. "Come on! It's more dangerous out there than in here. Think of all the snakes and jaguars ready to eat you. Might as well take your chances, hmm?"

In the end, he stepped inside. Perhaps he tripped. In any case, I didn't waste time. As if propelled by wings, I flew over and snatched him. I administered the curse and he went limp in my arms. I carried him inside and laid him on my bed.

3

DURING THE NIGHT, I prepared the mixture. One benefit of the jungle was that everything was to hand. I wandered into the moonlight. Despite being accustomed to the chirrups and croaks, that night, with the boy sleeping in my shack, they rang loud in my ears. In that moment, and for the first time in my life, I thought about what I'd done on Earth.

Perhaps I was feeling old and reflective. Six-hundred and fifty was old, even for a duende. I considered the powers unknown that had put me on Earth. Were they good or evil? Subjective or objective?

My earliest memory was lurking in dark places. Always near humans, but just out of sight. Just as a jaguar learnt to prey on smaller animals, I learnt to feast on human souls.

At one point, when I was about two-hundred years old, I experimented. I sat in my shack for years, refusing to steal another human's life force. And then one day I woke up, and I thought someone had stuck me with a knife. I shot out and stole an elderly fisherman's soul. Although frail and unsatisfying, it kept me from death.

Once the hunger subsided, around my three-hundredth year, I went about weaving my sail. No more human souls passed my lips. I weaned myself onto a diet of spiders and snakes.

The buzzes and chirrups of the jungle brought me back to the present. I rubbed my temples and rocked myself into action, needing to mix up the potion to extract the boy's soul.

Later that night, I trod through the undergrowth and picked up simple leaves and berries for the mixture, dropping them into my clay bowl.

Up above, the black sky took on a tinge of dark-blue and

morning light crept over the horizon. I trotted back and went about mashing up the potion.

When morning broke, it was ready. I fed it through the boy's pursed lips with a wooden spoon.

He juddered when the sour mixture met his tongue, but his eyes remained closed and he slept on. It would take about eight days for his young soul to leave his body and I would have the last part of my sail.

I sat on the step and watched the sun crawl into the sky. His family crossed my mind. Soon they'd be waking up. Had they noticed him missing the day before? If not, would they notice now?

When I re-entered the shack, he lay on his back with his eyes wide open. Floorboards groaning under my feet, I trod over and watched his little face. I had changed his life forever. He would never remember anything from now on. Even his memories were gone. All the skills he'd learnt, his friends' names, his mother's face.

Once I finished extracting the soul, I always returned the body —no more than an empty shell—to its people. That way, I reasoned, at least they had closure.

I leant over the bed and waved my hand across his eyes. Nothing. I strolled to the corner and picked up a coconut. With my bare hands, I cracked it open and dripped the milk into his mouth.

On the second day, I stumbled into loggers.

4

S TUMPS AS FAR as the eye could see—the loggers sat in a clearing drinking coffee and eating deep-fried snacks.

Cold realisation seeped in. The path to the village was exposed, no cover for a duende. Any day the wise man might stroll up to my shack. I backed up and returned home.

Deciding to get on with weaving the soul sail, I held one of the bottles to my ear, listening to it hum. Each bottle contained up to ten souls, bouncing about waiting for release. Sniffing the cork, I guessed there were about eight inside.

I readied my needle and thread and twisted the cork. Through the tiny gap, a soul slipped out. I batted the cork in and caught the floating soul with my needle, piercing it and drawing the thread. In my hand, I held the string and let it float, like a kite, toward the roof.

Behind me, the boy stirred. I jumped—all too aware humans were acutely tuned to detect souls. Breath bated, I drew the soul in and tied the loose thread round the table leg.

I touched his forehead. It singed my hand. Panic struck me. No way could I let him die. The modern age was closing in fast and I might never get another chance to trap a soul.

Heart in mouth, I threw open my medicine chest and withdrew a tiny bottle of antidote. Never used before, the ingredients remained active. My hands trembled as I brought the bottle to his lips and poured it in. I watched his Adam's apple bob as he drank.

Eyes blank, he coughed.

Ice rattled my lungs. How had I been so stupid, to let him drift so close to death? I might have to restart the whole process.

Outside, perhaps a hundred feet away, I heard human voices. I glanced out the door to see the loggers, treading toward me. Three of them. Two with axes and the other with a chainsaw.

My pulse quickened. Would they investigate my shack? I watched on. Although their eyes fell on my house, they quickly moved on—skirting my zone of influence. A pity really, I was looking forward to throwing a few spells.

After turning away from the window, I reached out and laid the boy on his back. On the table, I'd left some mixture. With a quick look at him, I decided he was ready. I spooned it into his mouth.

Once the bowl was empty, he slipped into convulsions. I continued to stitch my sail, one eye on him the whole time. When he settled down, I held my fingers to his throat and felt his faint pulse.

On the third day, the sail resembled a spectral flag rippling in an invisible wind. Four hundred souls. I worked through the night, stopping every few hours to check on the boy. When I slept, I didn't dare to let the thin thread out of my hand. I was alert to every grunt or turn the boy made in sleep.

Days trotted by and I counted off the souls, making notches in my table. I counted seven hundred. Before I knew it, it was the eighth day and the sail covered the entire ceiling.

On that day, he slept on as normal, breathing evenly and gently. I held my hand over his mouth, savouring the warm breaths leaking from his body. Placing one hand on his chin and the other on his top-lip, I wrenched open his mouth.

Inside, a greenish-white light glimmered in the darkness. His soul. It wasn't ready quite yet, but it would be soon. I laid a bottle alongside his bed.

Evening sighed over us and I finished the sail. Nine-hundred and ninety-nine souls hovered above our heads, a divine sheet. Only one until it was complete.

Twilight settled in.

Convinced something had gone wrong, I fidgeted. Why hadn't his soul escaped?

Mouth an inch open, he breathed evenly.

I crouched down beside him and uncorked the bottle, waiting.

The sun sank and the cabin fell into darkness. Hands shaking, I didn't dare light a candle. Then it came.

It lit up every blood vessel in his cheeks and snuck out through his lips—a pea-sized snatch of light. I whipped out the bottle.

With a plop, the soul squeezed through the bottleneck. It expanded into a long rectangle, making the glass shimmer green. I held up the bottle.

I fumbled for my needle and thread, and waited for the soul to realise it was trapped. It floated up gently and I speared it. At last, I had my sail. Warmth passed through me. I let the sail drift to the roof. A silver flash swept across it.

Intent on finding the nearest boat and floating up to celestial bliss, I made my way out.

Behind me, the boy coughed.

I turned.

5

THE BOY SAT UP STRAIGHT, rubbing his eyes and I knew I had to take him back to his people. He was no threat to me now, unable to communicate, let alone form words to describe the monster—me. Even if the villagers put two and two together, I would be flying up away from earth. Far out of reach from their rifles and curses. A dull itch, at the back of my mind, told me I had to return him, like all the others.

Still holding the sail, I snatched him by the wrist with my free hand and led him outside.

Smoke licked my nostrils and I pushed him ahead. He stumbled, but caught himself before he fell. The sail flew over our heads. Invisible to humans, only seen by duendes.

Paranoia seeped in. I considered what might happen if another duende spied a completed sail. Would he steal it from me?

When we reached the edge of the forest, I noticed the loggers' progress. Another day and they would have reached my shack. I flinched and trudged on.

In the dead of night, we arrived at the village.

Dogs lay sleeping, piled against the cabins' outside walls. One false move would send them barking and the villagers out.

I shoved the boy onwards, to his village. He staggered and stopped. I shoved him again. Once more, he took a couple of steps and then hesitated. Strange. Usually, when they saw the village, some instinct kicked in. A spark of recognition. And they walked off to their beds.

I gulped and took his hand. Taking care not to make a sound, I led him past sleeping dogs and into the village square, where I let go of his hand. "Go on! You're free."

He stood still, staring.

I shrugged. If the boy stayed there until morning, the villagers would find him. If he decided to drift into the woods, a jaguar would eat him. Having led him that far, my conscience was clean. Keeping him in sight, I walked back into the jungle.

His shoulders rose, his lungs ballooned and he let loose a blood-curdling scream, "Duende!"

I bolted between the trees.

6

THE SOUND of stamping feet and villagers' shouts pursued me.

I tripped over a root and crashed to the ground. I pulled myself up and ran on.

Soon, I'd led them all the way back to my cabin.

They screamed to one another, waking up all the animals. Monkeys screeched in the trees.

Which way was the river? I had no idea.

Torches blazed in the gaps between trees. My eyes darted along them, trying to work out where the attack would come. I ran back inside my influence, diving behind my shack.

A villager emerged into the clearing. Biting my tongue, I tied the thread attached to my sail around the cabin. Fire lit up his mouth and forehead, casting his eyes in shadow. He stood inches from my influence.

I leant back and prepared my hexes.

They spoke in hushed whispers. I strained to listen, but it didn't sound important. Fingers massaging my temples, I waited. A twinge shot up my spine. They were inside. I dived round the corner, ranting and raving spells. Purple and blue light splattered. A whiff of burning filled the air. Villagers dropped left, right and centre—clutching their throats and choking.

I stood to watch them die. Only one remained, a shadow watching from the trees. I strolled toward him, treading round the odd convulsing body. "Come out and fight!"

He stared back.

I reached the fringes of my influence. Human nature dictated this one would be in a hurry. Who could blame them? They had a tenth of the time I did. No time for taking stock, only time to act —the intelligent ones anyway.

He remained standing.

Growing impatient, I paced back and forth. "Come on!"

He stepped closer, revealing his face. It was the boy.

I stepped to the very edge of my influence.

All round me, the entire male population of the village lay dead, or dying. Wasn't he going to say something? Then I remembered he had no soul.

"What do you want?" I said. "Why couldn't you leave me in peace?"

His mouth moved. A gust of wind blew across the clearing, drowning out the words.

"What?"

He smiled.

A pang of terror rushed my brain. That wasn't right. He shouldn't have been able to display emotion. He was just a carcass, a husk blowing about in the breeze. Hadn't the potion done its work?

Anger poisoned my blood. Conscious of keeping my feet inside my influence, I reached out for him. It wasn't enough. I remained inches from him.

He didn't react.

Seeing the predicament, I swallowed. Something had to be done. I took a couple of steps back and charged.

I clattered into him, our bones colliding. He lay under me. I pinned his arms, either side of him. "What are you doing? You're going to spoil everything!"

Not even the flicker of an eyelid.

I slammed his wrists hard against the ground. "What? What is it?"

Someone groaned behind me. I looked back.

One of the villagers lay on his side, not quite dead. I gritted my teeth, preparing a curse. However, when I tried to act, I couldn't move. I looked down to see the boy had locked his legs round mine. My eyes widened and I tried to worm from his grasp. I was a sitting duck outside my influence.

The villager got to his feet and limped toward me, a ceremonial dagger clutched in his fist and hate in his eyes. I recognised him from before. It was the wise man.

Beyond him, I realised my shack lay in splinters. I had destroyed it in that flurry of magic and adrenalin. My soul sail floated up over the trees, like a second moon.

I squeezed my eyes shut. All was lost. I didn't have hundreds of years to weave another one.

The wise man stumbled on.

Desperate, I hoped he might slip and break his neck. But he remained sure-footed.

With a final effort, I tried to break free from the boy's grasp. Nothing. The image of my soul sail flying on the breeze, painted on the backs of my eyelids, sucked all the energy from my body.

Only a few yards away, a wicked grin sprung onto the wise man's face.

I gripped the boy close to me and waited for death.

GRAVEYARD

I NSIDE HIS GUARD BOOTH, Horace Stanfield leant back in the chair until his grey hair brushed up against the back wall. The electric heater and blanket kept him snug, while the steaming cup of hot chocolate warmed his hands. Photographs covered the walls all around him. The faces of his wife and son smiled back, reminders of better times.

The graveyard gate rattled.

Those damn kids coming in to cause trouble again. It made him want to vomit. Although they didn't pay him to watch the plots, only to dig, Horace had resolved to protect the dead months ago. The day he'd come in to find used condoms, cans of lager and his wife's stone covered in graffiti had convinced him the graveyard needed a security guard. He'd let her memory down—his wife's physical remainder. So, with the reverend's permission, he'd built this simple shed and taken up watch—better than going back to an empty house every night.

Horace dragged up his shirt sleeve and checked his watch. Three hours ago he'd finished the grave for tomorrow. He sighed then got to his feet. A jolt of pain shot through his left knee, making him wince.

On his way out, he picked up the air-rifle, resting against the doorpost next to the shovel. He whipped back the bolt then blew through the barrel. Dust rose into the air. A long time since he'd used it, but he was sick and tired of those kids. Someone needed to teach them a lesson.

He removed a pellet from his jacket pocket and dropped it inside. He snapped the chamber shut then stormed out the door.

In the moonlight, the gravestones stood to attention—ragged soldiers in a well-battered battalion. Horace turned up his collar and tightened the straps of his hat with earmuffs to protect his ears from the steady snowfall and fierce January wind.

Upon reaching the first junction, he paused to examine his two options. The first path presented the most direct route to the front gate, but no cover. If he went that way the kids would see him and escape before they were in range.

Glancing the other way sent a tingle through his veins. His elbow twitched and he almost dropped the gun. He didn't like to think about that route. The path itself was around a yard wide with a tall rusted iron fence on either side. It looped outwards, away from the town, skirting the frosted fields.

Many years ago, they'd dug out plots on that side. Those days, he took the route in the dawn and the dusk, but never at night. When he filled the last hole, he remembered his glee at never having to return—never having to revisit his wife's grave and never having to revisit the emptiness at its side, where his own body would be found one day. That was until the day the kids got in and forced him back there to clean up their mess.

One thing was for certain, though, they wouldn't expect him to come along that path. It emerged at the entrance through tangled branches. Most people didn't know it existed. He smiled. It would be the fright of their lives.

Horace took a deep breath and trod on, leaving fresh-prints in the snow behind him.

The first step was the hardest. Wasn't that what they said? Indeed, the thrill of the chase—a boyish rush—and the security of the gun held to his chest, pushed him on.

A tree rustled. He stopped dead and looked out into the darkness, pointing the gun in the direction of the sound.

A cat? A squirrel? Silence.

He let the gun slip back down to his side.

The graves thinned out and the trees thickened, hiding him

from the full moon and plunging him into darkness. The names on the stones were unfamiliar.

He stumbled, but regained his balance before falling. Looking back, he saw roots spilling out onto the path, half-hidden in the snow. He had to be more careful with his trailing left leg.

The field spread out ahead, open and empty, stretching away from him and into ever after. The image made him wonder why he'd never left town. Sure, he'd lived in the city for a couple of years in his youth, but he'd bolted back—with his tail between his legs— to the village where he grew up. He missed the familiar sights and sounds, the small hopes and dreams. And then it had become his prison, where he mourned his lost wife and son.

In the half-light from the moon, his breath came out in clouds. Horace stood still, listening to his breathing.

A peal of laughter.

Horace froze. No turning back. He was almost halfway to the entrance and wanted to jump those kids more than anything. Responsibility weighed on his mind like a block of lead. He thought about their unspeakable deeds: defacing gravestones, drinking on consecrated ground, feeling each other up. No respect for the dead.

Like a bear out of hibernation, he trudged through the snow dunes, scraping his arms on the branches that jutted out into the path. His heart beat hard against his ribcage as he rounded the corner.

Snow covered the grave and the top of the stone, but the front remained legible—the lettering proud and clear. At least they hadn't been at his wife's plot tonight. That much he had to be thankful for. He crouched down so her name sat in his line of sight, the closest he could get to looking her in the eye.

ROSEMARY G. STANFIELD

"It's been a while." Horace glanced around, not quite feeling alone. "Sorry I don't visit more often."

The graveyard stood reverent to their meeting. The wind dropped and the branches stayed still. Even the delinquents made no sound.

"I promise, after tonight, I'll bring you flowers every day." Horace straightened up then wiped a tear from the corner of his eye. "It's just." He paused then his eyes fell on the empty space to the side of her grave and his heart emptied. "I find it hard, after what happened. I'm so—"

A *crash* followed by screams of laughter.

His blood ran cold. The little bastards. If his son had lived, would he have had the same disrespect? No. Horace would've beaten it out of him, if he'd had to.

Taking the gun in his hands, Horace whispered to the grave, "I've got to go." Horace struggled to his feet, feeling his chest drew tight. As he trotted along the path, he clipped the safety catch off the gun then lurched out into the clearing by the front gate.

Nothing.

Panting with effort, Horace's eyes strained to strip back the darkness. When he composed himself, he slunk back up the main path—dejected at having missed the kids again.

When the moon came out from behind its cloud, it revealed everything. Taking his opportunity, Horace ran his eyes across the whole of the graveyard: the principal paths, the rows upon rows of gravestones and his guard booth at the other end.

Another outbreak of laughter.

A cold feeling gripped his stomach, passed up through his heart and lungs then entered his brain. He spun around, his eye level with the rifle sight. If he couldn't see them from where he stood, they had to be *on* the graves.

Anger rose inside him, pushing back the coldness. He bounded up the path to his guard booth, rifle primed, ready for any child that strayed from its hiding place. Peering between the lines of gravestones, he tried to catch sight of a clue: the flash of a t-shirt, the flurry of snow, footprints—but nothing.

Horace reached his guard booth then stopped. "Come out!" His words bounced around the trees then the night swallowed them up. "I'll get the lot of you! This isn't your place." His voice cracked under the strain of words. "You can't come in." A tear rolled down his face and dropped to his feet. Deep down, he knew the kids had gone and they'd be back tomorrow. Why did he bother?

Something grabbed him around the chest.

Panicked, he looked down, but saw nothing. Invisible hands bound him. "Let me go!" His arm lost its strength and the rifle slipped from his hands, burying itself in a bone-white snow dune. The sharp pain in his left knee grew and grew. Then his knee buckled and he toppled to the ground.

Frustrated at letting his guard down, Horace lay on his side. His eyes flitted around the scenery. Where would the attack come from? He screwed up his face in pain and cried uncontrollably, pounding his fists against the snow. Trying to get to his feet, he found he couldn't—like someone had attached a boulder to his left knee as some cruel joke.

"*Dad?*"

Horace turned his head, but didn't see anything. He tried to wrench open his eyes, but the tears stung him. Was there a person looking back at him from that tree? Hard to tell, but he did see something.

Horace grasped for the gun, but it was out of reach. The person in the trees refused to come into focus. Defeated, Horace bowed his head. "What do you want from me?"

Footsteps crunched across the snow. "I want to take you with me."

"Where?"

A pause. "To where she is."

Horace gulped then nodded. "Okay."

A warm hand touched his face, but Horace didn't dare look up. The hand's touch warmed him and his tension shod away. The confidence returned. Confidence he hadn't felt since he was a teenager . . . before the weight of the world crushed him.

"You've done such a wonderful job," the figure said. "She's safe now."

"How can you be sure?"

"Dad?" The figure paused. "Look at me."

Horace stared at the ground. "I can't."

"Of course you can."

Gradually, Horace tilted his head back and took in the figure. It was Matthew, his son. They'd never found his body after the accident, but here he was! The boy he'd never buried. Matthew's form filled out now. Nothing about him shimmered.

"What happens now?" Horace said.

"You come with me."

"Is she there . . . your mother?"

Matthew nodded.

Alarmed, Horace glanced around—still worried the kids were out there somewhere, defiling people's memories. "But who'll look after the graveyard. Mum's grave?"

"Dad, please, you're an old man now. Someone else can take on the responsibility." Matthew glanced around as if someone might be listening.

Horace moved his leg. No pain. He got to his feet with his liberated knee. "I'm fine, look!" He held his arms in the air and, forgetting himself in the sensation, did a little jig. "I don't know what you did to me, but I'm cured."

Matthew smiled.

Horace's face fell. "I'm dead, aren't I?" With a new appreciation for the world, Horace looked around. The world he was about to leave behind. "The graveyard will be safe?"

"Of course." Matthew held out his arm. "You're going to see Mum soon. Come on."

"Really?"

"Yes. I'm your carrier. It's my job to take you to her."

Taking Matthew's arm, Horace felt his chest lift. When Horace spoke, his words seemed to float in bubbles around his head, "We'll be together?"

"You and Mum will be, yes."

Horace frowned. "But you won't be with us?"

"I'm left to wander the void. I can never go with you and Mu—"

"Is it because we never found your body?" Horace paused. "Because I never buried you?"

"Those are the rules."

Despite the neutral look on Matthew's face, Horace sensed Matthew's regret. "I'm sorry."

"You couldn't help it."

They ascended slowly. One or two inches, at first, then faster. Soon, everything spun out of control and white light reigned.

LAST BIRCH STANDING

TREE STUMPS SURROUNDED JACOB, as far as he could see. Silence. No birds in the overcast skies or animals running across the muddy ground. Grey pervaded everything.

He whipped back the cord and the chainsaw spluttered to life. Kyle, his co-worker, sat up on one of the branches filming on his mobile. Jacob slashed into the air and Kyle gave him a thumbs up.

Fifty feet back, their supervisor called through his megaphone, "All right, boys! Let's get this over and done with. No drama. Just like we talked about!"

Kyle clambered down.

Holding the chainsaw level with his chest, Jacob wondered whether his name would go down in history. Jacob Hatherter, the man who had cut down the last tree on Earth. Jubilation passed through him. He looked along the spinning blades—him and the tree.

Vibrations shook his muscles. It took all his strength to keep the blade straight and go right through the trunk. Branches rustled and the tree fell. Kyle and the supervisor cheered.

Grinning ear-to-ear, he mopped his brow and looked out over the horizon. He held his hand to shield his eyes from the setting sun. Someone stood there. A shiver ran through his bones, like someone had stolen all the warmth from his body.

He squinted. It was a man wearing a grey suit. Just as he took in the image, there was a flash. He covered his eyes and when he looked back, the man was gone.

His supervisor slapped him on the back.

A jolt ran through his frozen nerves.

The supervisor revealed a bottle of champagne. "Well done, lad. Excellent job. Nice clean cut." He popped the cork and foam flowed down the sides, dripping down his hands. After taking a swig, he passed the bottle to Kyle. "Look around boys! This'll all be hemp a year from now."

Kyle drank long and deep, leaving the bottle half-full when he handed it to Jacob.

Jacob took it in his numb hands. When he took a sip, the alcohol didn't warm the coldness in his stomach—it just made him want to vomit.

2

DEFENCE SECRETARY Pearson's personal assistant, Dan Cleverly, jumped from his seat. Two orange lights blinked on the printer and the spool spun. He turned back. "You've pressed print, have you, sir?"

Pearson looked up over the top of his half-moon glasses. His gut flopped out over his belt. "Yes, Cleverly. Do you need some help?"

"No paper coming out, sir. Lights are flashing."

He came over.

Oniony breath and musky odour wafted into Dan's nostrils. He knew Pearson didn't have a clue about machines—the more cables, the worse.

Pearson smacked the printer.

Dan winced. "Sir?"

Pearson gave the machine another *whack*. "Bloody thing!" He swung his arm back for a third blow.

"Sir!" He dashed between Pearson and printer.

His hand hung in the air. "What, boy?"

"I think it's out of paper."

"Whatever brings you to that conclusion?"

"The lights, I suppose." He scratched his head. "Look at the paper tray. It's empty."

Pearson glanced down. "Bloody technocrap."

"I'll go and get some from the stock cupboard, shall I?"

"Yes, my boy." He strutted back to his desk.

Dan searched the cupboard. He paused at each shelf and ran his eyes across the items. When he reached the bottom, and had found no paper, he stood back to take in the vista. He put his hands on his hips. Where was it?

He got down on his hands and knees to check the bottom

shelf. Cobwebs and discarded plastic covers, but no paper. He'd have to return to Pearson empty handed and that wouldn't go down well.

On the way back to the office, an idea struck him. Why didn't he go upstairs to the Ministry of Culture and dip into their paper stash? He knew the disciplinary measures awaiting those who stole office supplies from fellow departments, but it was that or face Pearson. Without further deliberation, he went upstairs. If anyone asked him what he was doing, he would say he was getting a cup of coffee.

The Ministry of Culture kept their stationery cupboard the same way the Culture Secretary kept himself—tattered and covered in pieces of food. On the second shelf to his left, was a smooth white packet of paper. After looking up and down the corridor, he stuffed it into his jacket.

Back in the office, he handed over the paper with a grin.

Frowning, Pearson turned the package over in his hands. "Where'd you get this?"

"From the stationery cupboard."

Pearson turned red. "Liar!"

Dan's pulse quickened.

Pearson held up the packet label:

Ministry of Culture – NOT FOR INTERDEPARTMENTAL USE.

Dan swallowed. He'd thought Pearson would've liked the gesture. After all, he was always going on about the Culture Secretary.

Then Pearson's frown disappeared and a grin broke through. He clapped him on the back. "Good work, my boy! Get at those bloody fairies." He held out his hand. "Letter opener."

Dan's hands shook as he delved into the drawer. He removed a cow bone letter opener.

Muttering something incomprehensible, Pearson made a slit in the plastic and ripped it from the package of paper. He held the paper out to him.

Dan laid the paper in the tray and pressed the button. The sheets shot through. Once printed, he collected up the sheets and brought them over.

Pearson thumbed through the pages. His eyes widened. "Jesus."

"Sir?"

Pearson dropped the papers onto his desk. "I've got an associate on the other side of town who should see this."

"But, sir, isn't that confidential? Not to leave Ministry premises, and all that?"

Pearson grumbled and then scribbled something on a scrap of paper. He attached it to the documents. "Do it quickly. Get it across there and don't stop for anything."

Outside, a fresh December breeze blew. Dan turned up his collar. Under his right arm, the documents slipped and he grabbed them before they dropped to the ground. His eyes searched ahead of him. The pavements were packed with Christmas shoppers. He struggled against them, clutching the documents to his chest.

He decided to avoid them by going through the park. He passed through the gates and walked past a homeless man sitting on a bench, huddled in blankets.

Dan's phone vibrated in his pocket. He jumped. Taking a deep breath, he reached in and withdrew it. "Hello?"

"Dan? Dan?" It was Pearson. "Are you there?"

"Yes, sir. What's the matter?"

"The documents! Did you deliver the documents?"

He glanced round. "No, not yet."

"It's about the paper!"

"What about it?"

"Apparently that was a special order, taken from the last tree on Earth, or something."

Scrunching his forehead, he glanced back at the homeless man. "So?"

"So! The Culture Secretary was just here, going absolutely bat shit! He's threatening to get the PM on me. He caught you on camera, Dan!"

Dan's lip wobbled. "But whatever did they want that paper—"

"I don't know! To put in a fucking museum or something! The point being, get rid of the documents, dump them somewhere. No evidence, no case!"

"Where? Where do I take them?"

In the background, he heard, what he assumed to be, breaking crockery. "Anywhere!" Pearson screamed. The phone clicked off.

Dan's heart pounded in his throat. He looked round the park for a rubbish bin. There were none. Numb with fear, his eyes rested on the homeless man. He thrust the documents at him. "Take them!"

The homeless man leafed through the papers and then laid them down beside him. He shucked off the blankets to reveal a grey suit.

Dan stood shell-shocked, mouth agape.

"You know where this comes from?" The homeless man held out an accusatory finger, pointing at the paper.

"Oh, erm. What?" Dan glanced round for help.

The homeless man got to his feet and laid his hand on his chest. "I want your soul."

Coldness ran through Dan, like someone had blasted him with a freeze-ray. He stumbled backward onto the ground, feeling empty inside. The homeless man towered over him.

Dan felt for grip and managed to pull himself to his feet. He bolted from the park and back to the Ministry.

ANDERS FILED HIS NAILS while watching a pair of heavyset men lay his birch cabinet down. One of the men glanced at him. "How's that, sir?"

He put the file to one side and closed an eye. "Slide it a bit to the right."

The men made the correction. The same man looked to him for approval.

Anders waved his arm and smiled. "That'll do."

The man nodded. He and his accomplice left the office.

Anders leant back in his leather chair and admired the cabinet made from the last tree on Earth. In the future, it would be worth an absolute fortune—not that he'd sell it, of course. Things like these gave a man an extra air of dignity and importance. This morning, he had merely been the CEO of a multi-billion pound technology company, but now he was something much more.

However, he was missing something. How would he back up the claim that this cabinet was made from the last tree on Earth? What evidence could he supply? After a moment's thought, he came up with the answer—a photograph and a signed declaration. He would need to track down the fence, the man who had sold him the item.

He touched the intercom button and his secretary, Hazel, spoke, "Yes, Mr Morchek?"

"What's the schedule looking like for this afternoon?"

"You've got the men from HiSystems then the woman from LoUncts coming in."

"Cancel them."

"Certainly, sir. Is that all?"

"See if you can track down the seller of my cabinet."

"Ok, sir." The intercom clicked off.

He looked out over the cityscape. The late-afternoon smog rose up from the streets in brown waves.

The red intercom light flashed. He blinked. Impossible that Hazel had tracked down the man so quickly. He clicked 'Receive.'

"Sir? I've found the cabinet importer."

"Excellent. Send out an invitation." He let go of the button and crossed the room. The intercom flashed again.

"No, sir. He's here."

"What?"

"Yes."

He tilted his head and marvelled at the coincidence. "Right-oh, tell him I'll be right there." He clicked off, already having second thoughts. Was this man clean? It wouldn't do to get involved with the mob. He'd have to get the guy in-and-out quickly—he didn't want people talking behind his back, suggesting he was crooked.

After sliding open the drawer, he ran his fingers across his variety of ties. He chose an emerald-green silk one then slipped it round his neck. He stroked the cabinet on his way out and fixed a smile on his face.

In the waiting area, a grey-suited man flipped through one of the high-end magazines on the coffee table.

Anders walked across the room. "Anders Morchek." He held out his hand. "Pleased to meet you."

The grey-suited man put the magazine down and craned his neck. For a moment, he didn't think the man would accept his handshake. Then he broke out into a smile, speckled with gold filings, and shook his hand.

A shiver ran up Anders's spine. It was like touching a block of ice. The smile slipped from his face. The man clutched tighter. Trying to peel his hand free, Anders spoke through clenched teeth, "This way, please."

The man released his hand.

In the office, the man crossed his legs—resting his foot on the opposite knee cap. He produced a gold lighter from his pocket and tapped it on the side of his scuff-marked shoe. "Do you mind if I smoke, Mr Morchek?"

Something deeply unsettled him about this man. Was it his cold handshake? Was it the loose skin hanging off his neck, like a reptile? Remembering the question, he shook his head.

The man sucked on his cigarette and puffed out smoke. "How's the cabinet?"

Anders squirmed then forced a smile. "Good, thank you. Very pleased with it."

The man glanced round the office.

Was he pricing up his possessions, considering a robbery? He rocked forward, placing his hands flat on the table and eyed the man. "So, Mr . . ."

"Elnwick." His eyes were like bottomless pits.

"Mr Elnwick. I was wondering if you might be able to help me."

He grunted and blew out more smoke, making Anders cough. "Not sure. What can you do for me?"

"Right. Money?"

He pouted.

"It's about the cabinet. Do you happen to have a photograph of the tree, you know, before it was cut down?"

Elnwick held up the butt of his cigarette, indicating a need to find somewhere to stub it out.

"Ah, ashtray?" Anders clicked the intercom and requested one from Hazel.

Elnwick snorted. "I happen to have some evidence, yes. I was there, in fact."

"Really?"

"Uh-huh." Elnwick looked ready to stub the butt out on the desk, just as Hazel came in—a porcelain bowl clutched in her hands. She laid it on the desk and, with a look of disappointment, he dropped the butt inside.

The butt rested in the bowl, the perverted grey against pearl white. Anders never kept ashtrays about the place and abhorred smokers. No-one had ever had the audacity to smoke in his office.

Elnwick leant back in the chair and removed another cigarette from inside his jacket. "What can you pay me with?"

Anders's forehead crumpled. He had a team of negotiators to do this sort of thing for him. He hadn't discussed prices in years. "Same rate as the cabinet?"

"How about your soul?"

Anders stared. "I beg your pardon?"

Elnwick lit up another cigarette. "Your soul."

"What do you mean?"

"Well, I get you the photograph and you give me your soul. It's really quite simple."

"No, thank you. I'll pay in cash."

Elnwick took a drag and held the smoke in. "I want your soul." He breathed out an impossibly long plume of smoke. "That's why I came here today."

Anders twitched. How had he let Elnwick dominate the room? He reached for the intercom. "Why my soul? What's so special about mine?"

"It would be easy to transfer."

"I find that hard to believe."

"Take your finger off the button."

A cold wave passed over Anders and he realised he was shaking. He snatched his hand back and gulped. "Is it . . . painful?"

"What?"

"Giving you my soul."

Elnwick snorted and dropped his half-cigarette in the ashtray. "No. Not really."

What could it hurt, if it got the man out of his office? "Tell me what to do, and I'll do it."

"Get a piece of paper."

Anders reached inside his desk drawer and produced a pad. He slid it across the desk.

"No." Elnwick laid his palm on the pad and slid it back. "You write."

Sweat trickled down Anders's back. He picked up a pen.

Elnwick leant forward. His breath stank of stale smoke and fish guts. "Write the date." He breathed in deep through his nostrils. "Now write, 'I hereby bequeath my soul to James G. Elnwick.'"

Despite his fear, Anders copied the dictation in his florid handwriting and glanced up—like a sheepdog awaiting a command.

"Sign it."

Anders sketched out the curves of his signature, finishing with the zigzagged 's' he'd worked on for so long as a young man.

"Good. Now the blood." Elnwick dipped his hand into his jacket pocket and removed a giant silver-bladed knife, which he laid on the desk.

Anders glared at the blade. How the hell had that cleared security? His eyes widened. Shaking, he took up the blade. He hesitated, before making a neat diagonal slit across his thumb. Ignoring the sting, he pressed his thumb to the paper—leaving a neat, crimson print.

Elnwick snatched up the paper then blew on the wet blood. He folded the paper into quarters then slipped it in his pocket. He got to his feet and walked to the door.

Anders stirred from his daze. "What now?"

Elnwick turned. A strange red tinge flashed across his eyes. Would he rush him, blade in hand? He smiled and laid his hand on the doorknob. "I'll bring the evidence tonight."

Anders shuddered. No way did he want to see this man again.

He could hardly speak, but he got the words out. "No, I . . . I don't want it."

"Very well. Pity."

When the door shut behind him, Anders breathed a sigh of relief. He reached for a handkerchief and wiped the sweat from his forehead. Across the room, the cabinet remained. He had to get it out.

Anders pressed the buzzer. "Hazel?"

"Yes, sir. Is something the matter?"

"I want them to take the cabinet away."

"Right away, sir."

"Oh, and Hazel?"

"Sir?"

"Tell the head of security he's fired."

"Yes, sir."

He released his finger from the intercom and eyed the cabinet. It was like someone had dunked him in a stone well filled to the brim with ice.

4

WIND BLEW Margaret Matthews's grey hair all over as the paramedics whipped open the ambulance doors. Lying back on the stretcher, she observed the *Stanley Grove Private* sign pass above. She exhaled. Just like coming home.

The automatic doors flew open and the scent of lavender seeped up her nostrils. On each side, a young male paramedic guided her along the hallway.

They came to a stop and one of the paramedics leant over. He had a handsome face and floppy blond hair, like a golden-retriever. "Here we are, madam. The doctor will be with you shortly to see about your arm."

She scrunched up her features. "Thank you kindly."

Grinning at everyone who passed by, she noticed the oil painting on the wall—a picture of an old country house on a lake. She lost herself in the colours, sweeping back-and-forth—dark-greens and blues. Almost off the canvas stood a dark forest. She peered closer. What was that? If she wasn't mistaken, it was a thin man, dressed in a grey suit, walking into the forest. It seemed out of place. A gnawing itch sprang up in her afflicted arm. She scratched and then winced in pain.

The sound of steps echoed through the corridor and a doctor, dressed in a pale-blue lab coat, approached her. He clutched a thin brass clipboard and smiled. "My name's Doctor Carmine. How are you today, Mrs. Matthews?"

"Good thank you, doctor. Well . . ." She looked down. "Apart from the arm."

"We'll soon sort that out."

"I hope so, doctor."

He wheeled her into a room and laid his clipboard on an examination bed. He drew up a chair alongside her. "Now, I' m just going to give you a quick examination." He placed his hands on her arm.

Searing pain stabbed her temples. She squirmed.

He looked up. "Does that hurt?"

She nodded.

"All right. Just one more test." He twisted her arm.

She tried to maintain her composure, but the pain got too much to bear. "Stop!"

He released her arm. "Oh, dear. I am sorry. I think it may be broken."

She massaged her arm with her good hand. "Really? It was just a tap I didn't think—" Her eyes looked to the painting on the wall, similar in style to the one in the corridor. The same grey-suited man sat slouched up against a wall.

"Mrs Matthews?"

She looked back at him and winced. "Sorry, doctor, I slipped away for a moment."

He eyed her closely and scribbled something on his clipboard. "Let's get you to x-ray." He assumed his familiar smile and got to his feet.

He held out his hand and she accepted it. She sat back in the wheelchair. Now she felt silly, she didn't need a wheelchair—it was her arm that was broken, not her legs. However, before she had a chance to point this out, he wheeled her into the corridor.

Behind her, the wheels squeaked and the doctor breathed heavily. Her eyes took in the oil paintings on either side. Although she couldn't be sure, she thought she saw the same grey-suited figure in each. Each time closer to the frame. She wanted to tell the doctor to stop, but maybe he'd think she was crazy—and he seemed such a nice man.

Like windmill blades, his voice came and went. She needed to tear her eyes from the paintings and concentrate on the words to understand.

He leant over her, body odour thick in her nostrils. ". . . Did you do it?"

She tilted her head back. "Sorry, doctor?"

"I was asking what happened."

"Oh. A car hit me while I was crossing the road."

He stopped the wheelchair and came round to face her. His face was sincere. "Did you tell the paramedics?"

"No, I didn't see the need."

"The car drove off?"

"No, they stopped and helped me to my feet, quite gentlemanly of them really."

"Would you like me to report the incident to the police? You may be entitled to compensation, this sort of thing might go to court for all I know."

She held up her good hand. "Really, does someone who can afford treatment at Stanley Grove need compensation?"

Still crouched on his haunches, he said, "That's not what concerns me. They are accountable to the law. They can't just go round knocking people over."

Her cheeks flushed. "Please, doctor, I have no intention of prosecuting those men." She pulled an eyelash from her cheek. "I was more concerned about the lovely cabinet that fell off the back of the van. Smashed to smithereens."

"All right." He resumed wheeling.

From behind the screen, the x-ray technician beamed at her. "Good afternoon, madam, this won't take long, I promise." He patted the bed. "If you'd be so kind as to lie down."

She tried to get up from the wheelchair, but a hot feeling in both legs stopped her and she dropped back down.

The technician rushed round the screen and grabbed her arm. "Are you okay, madam? Would you like me to call an assistant?"

She stared at him, unable to understand how she'd got there. Then it all came back. Above the x-ray bed was another oil painting. Again, it had the familiar grey-suited figure. Where had she seen him before?

The machines whirred in her ears as she lay back—letting the camera scan her withered bones. Now she remembered the man in the paintings. After the crash. He'd helped her up from the road, taken her across to the other side. She shivered then looked back at the painting. It must've been a coincidence.

The camera swooped away and the technician came round the screen. "All done." He indicated the door with his hand. "Your doctor is waiting outside. He'll let you know the results of the scan."

She nodded and paced across the room, ignoring the wheelchair.

Doctor Carmine waited with head bowed and hand on chin. Upon seeing her, he brushed off his serious face and smiled. "How did it go?"

"Oh, fine." She felt a little faint. She didn't want to look to the walls for fear she'd see the grey-suited man staring back from yet another painting.

"Let me escort you to the waiting area." He held out his arm and she looped hers through his.

Three leather sofas, a glass coffee table and a large flat screen TV occupied the waiting room. There were no paintings.

He patted her on the arm. "I'll bring the results to you when they're ready."

"Thank you, doctor." She sat down with a magazine. Her eyes barely grazed the glossy surface.

After about twenty minutes, Doctor Carmine poked his head round the door frame. "The results are ready, madam."

Behind him, she saw the wheelchair. He indicated the seat with his hand.

She walked past without sitting in it. "Where am I needed, doctor?"

"Plaster Room. Your arm is broken."

And so they headed on.

The plaster machine hummed away, drowning her thoughts in static. She was glad. She wanted to get out of the hospital, away from those paintings.

The nurse switched off the machine. "You're lucky, you know? This cast is made from one of the last batches of forest."

"Really? How horrific."

Open-mouthed as she went about her work, the nurse shook her head. "Haven't you heard they're planting hemp? It's a wonder crop." She concentrated on the cast, making it smooth. "To think we wasted so much time wondering about legalities and other such nonsense, when the answer was there all along."

She swallowed, staring over the nurse's shoulder at the painting. The grey-suited man filled the frame. Her mouth went numb. "I . . . like trees."

After the plaster had been fitted, Doctor Carmine led her to the main entrance of *Stanley Grove*, his hand in the small of her back. "You're sure I can't offer you a lift back home? It's part of the service after all."

"Quite sure. I'll take a taxi home."

"Very well. I hope you get well soon. The secretary will call you in the course of the next week to check how you're getting on and to arrange your next appointment."

"Goodbye, doctor."

He bowed and went back into the hospital.

She looked out at the day spread out in front of her. No bird-song, sweet scents or greenery to take her mind off the grey sprawl. What had they done to the planet? As she walked toward the main road, a car drew up and the grey-suited man jumped out.

Eyes wide, she stepped back. Her breath caught in her throat. "Wha—what do you want from me?"

He smiled. "Your soul."

"Why?"

"All those stocks you bought in logging." He nodded. "That cast on your arm. It looks like they've come back to haunt you."

"Bu—But—"

He held his finger to her lips and all the warmth drained from her body.

THE DEVIL & THE DISHWATER

I

THE ODOUR WAS ACIDIC, biting and gut-churning.

It smelled kind of like burned rubber. And kind of also like a great big hunk of manure. The taste got to the back of the mouth. Seemed to rub up against the skin. Bring all the hairs up nice and erect. And it was like it brought on a ringing of the ears too.

Nothing about the kitchen sink was good news.

That was to be taken for granted.

Terrence armed himself with a pair of canary-yellow washing-up gloves. He brought them flush onto his hands with a smart *snap* of rubber, and set his mind to the task stretching out before him.

Last night it had been observed that the egg-yolk-sized gunk about the plughole had turned a peachy colour, and the unanimous decision had been taken that someone had to go in there.

And, after the drawing of straws, that someone had turned out to be Terrence.

And so here he was.

Face to face with, if not certain death, then no doubt new levels of pain and disease as yet unseen in the developed world.

Or so went the theory about the student household.

Terrence held back for a long while. Just staring at the odious little patch of mould. Studying it as if he was back in the lab, back on campus. As if this was just another sample for him to poke and prod at.

Now, though, out of context . . . or, to be more exact, in his *own* context, the mould seemed almost totally insuperable.

It had been a fix in any case, Terrence was sure of it. And if he'd have had the proof, managed to work out just *how* his housemates might've fixed the pulling of straws, conspired against him so that *he* would be the one to go through with the task he would . . . well, most likely, he would have done it anyway.

Because Terrence was *nice* like that.

And *nice* people did things to help others.

Like cleaning horrible mould from plugholes. Sparing others from doing so.

His parents had always told him that he *had* to be *nice*.

No point pussyfooting around. Might as well get on with it. Get it through with once and for all. The prospect of the task would only get worse . . . was that another of those clichés his parents had told him once upon a time?

. . . Jesus, look at him now, even *that* was a cliché.

He was like a machine.

A very *nice*, very *boring* machine.

He grabbed for the hairy, metal scouring pad. Caught a sparkle of the bright kitchen lights in its surface. He took a deep breath . . . then remembered the horrific stench, and nearly brought his fish-and-chip dinner back up.

He kept it down.

But it was close.

Nothing for it now, though. Just better to get it over with. Not to even think about it. That was the best way to face it. Just *not even* think about it.

But that was much easier said than done.

Right.

Hot tap on.

Gushing down.

Check.

Steam rising.

Making contact with the gunk.

And . . . *Oh!*

For goodness' sake, the stench was just intolerable.

Terrence should've known better. His housemates had all tried that trick. The *hot* water trick. The trick that had failed over and over again. Just made it worse in fact.

Seemed to feed the gunk. Make it bigger if anything.

And now, just looking at it now, *staring* at it, Terrence was almost certain that he could see it growing before his eyes. Staking its claim to escape the whole sink.

Peachy, and furry, and revolting. And in need of being wiped away.

He clung tighter to the scouring pad, feeling its hairy, rough form even through the washing-up gloves, and then he took a deep breath and moved on in.

He was within a hair's breadth when he hesitated.

The hot water was still flowing. The water still slicking into the mould.

For some reason it felt like something was holding him back.

Stopping him from administering the coup de grâce.

And then he thought about just how stupid it was to think of wiping away a smear of mould in such florid terms.

He *really* needed to get out more.

The hot steam clouded his glasses, made them run with little channels of condensation. It was kind of like the time when he'd been camping, and it had rained the entire trip. Only the reverse this time . . . considering that he was *inside* and this was *hot* air, not cold.

Another deep breath, and then he dabbed at the mould with the scouring pad.

Just once.

Trying it out.

And then again.

Harder this time.

Yes, it was coming out now. He could see the mould coming

away from the kitchen sink. Squidging out its peachy colour onto the scouring pad, in any case.

A little more.

Just a little more.

He lost his previous inhibitions and really put his back into it.

Jabbed the scouring pad downwards, firmly, and made rigid scrubbing motions.

Back and forth, back and forth, back and forth.

With every motion more of the mould coming away.

Or was it?

He paused for a moment, wiping the perspiration forming on his forehead with the back of his washing-up glove. The steam from the hot tap billowed up and out of the sink, and it was something like being in a steam room . . . though the smells certainly weren't as neutral as they were, in theory, in a steam room. In fact, if he'd been served steam like that in a health club—if he could've afforded the membership—he would've damn well asked for his money back.

He looked down at his work. At that rampant fudge of peach-coloured mould lining the base of the sink, and then, and he was quite sure of it—certain, in fact—he saw it give a profound sigh.

2

THE AIR WENT SUDDENLY COLD. Then got hot again. His heart seemed to hammer against his tonsils, to throb in his eardrums, and the acrid stench of the soap stripped all other scents out from his nostrils. He could taste that soap as if someone had flushed it through his mouth. Like someone had stuffed a bar of soap in between his lips . . . or squirted in a handsome helping of washing-up liquid . . . and then tied a rag over his mouth, to stop him spitting it out.

Terrence never would've believed that mould could sigh if he hadn't seen it with his own two eyes. But the fact remained that he had. He had *seen* this patch of peach-coloured mould that had hung around in their kitchen sink for weeks—months?—actually give a sigh.

He blinked a couple of times. Maybe it was the steam, getting to his head, making him go totally crazy. Maybe it was because he'd spent the day in the lab, on campus, going slowly crazy over pipettes and test tubes and Bunsen burners while the sun beamed down on his oblivious peers, all stretched out on the lawns, tanning themselves, getting *drunk*, laughing and joking.

All arts students, no doubt.

Terrence stayed right where he was, as if the mould might be armed. As if he should really be cautious before he scoped out the true abilities of this patch of mould.

Know your enemy . . . wasn't that what they said?

Why did he think this patch of mould was his enemy?

How had *that* thought got stuck in his brain?

What had prompted it?

. . . He guessed the scientist in him just wouldn't let him stop asking questions.

C'est la vie.

He watched the glob of peachy mould. More carefully this time. As if he was trying to scope out its weaknesses. Or maybe that was just what he told himself when he knew that the true *real* reason was that he wanted to see whether or not it would sigh a second time.

It stayed where it was. Apparently static.

Off in the distance, he heard a key crunch into the lock of the front door. He heard a rumbling voice followed by feminine giggles out on the front step. And then, a moment later, the creak of hinges followed by the scuffing of feet on the welcome mat—just about as fuzzy and beaten up as the scouring pad he still clutched in his hand.

And then the voices themselves.

Clear and echoing down the hallway.

". . . Well, this is the place, for what it's worth."

Paul. His housemate. *Bald* Paul as Terrence had christened him, though only in his mind.

He wouldn't *dare* say that to his face.

For some reason he had caught wind of the fact that Bald Paul wasn't bald by choice, he had heard it off someone—though he forgot who now—who'd said that Bald Paul had some kind of an illness that meant he couldn't grow hair at all.

Terrence had never thought to follow it up.

"Nice, really, nice," the girl's voice came along the hallway. "Have to say I'm impressed."

Their footsteps scuffed along the bedraggled hallway carpet and Terrence prayed that they'd just head up to Bald Paul's bedroom, take care of their carnal desires, and leave him in peace down here . . . in just about as much peace as he *could* have with this blob of mould.

Their footsteps got louder. Coming in the direction of the kitchen.

"Wanna drink?" Bald Paul said to his date.

Terrence actually screwed his eyes up this time and *did* mutter a little prayer under his breath.

"All right," the girl replied.

He let loose a muted swearword but had no time to shuck the washing-up gloves before Bald Paul ploughed in through the doorway to the kitchen, pinned a grin across his thick, pulsating purplish lips, his cherubic cheeks, and said, "Thought everyone else was out."

"Nah," Terrence said, trying to smile, but having it come out as more of a wince. He nodded to the sink. To the patch of mould still festering there. "You know, still taking care of this."

Bald Paul flashed his eyebrows.

Or flashed what might've been—optimistically—termed his eyebrows.

Bald Paul glanced back over his shoulder.

Terrence saw the girl wander in.

She had blond hair and wore a white top over a pair of faded black jeans. Her skin was fair and poked out at her shoulders, cleavage, and tummy.

She fixed a pout onto her lips, and aimed a deeply disinterested glance at Terrence.

"Gotta see this," Bald Paul said, "It's just about the most horrible thing I've seen in my entire life."

Terrence flipped off the hot tap and took a step to one side, making room for the two of them to take in the exposition. Or what was turning into an exposition.

Terrence whipped his glasses off his face and went about cleaning off the condensation with the hem of his t-shirt. His reasoning, whenever he couldn't be bothered to go and dig out his glasses case—the lint-free cloth that came with them—was that the hem of his t-shirt was most likely the cleanest part. Less likely to scratch them. That was what he told himself, anyway.

As the girl approached the sink, she gave him a thicker pout before looking at just where Bald Paul was pointing so excitedly. "See that? Isn't it just *sick*, yeah?"

"What is it?" the girl said.

"Dunno, some kind of mould, I guess," Bald Paul said, and then shot Terrence a glance. "You're a scientist, don't you know?"

Terrence shrugged. "Not that kind of scientist."

The two of them, the girl and Bald Paul, stared at the mould for a fair few more seconds, and then, Bald Paul clapped Terrence on the shoulder and said, "Well, good luck, eh?" before grabbing hold of the girl's hand and leading her from the kitchen, apparently forgetting all about the promised drink.

And that just left Terrence to do battle with Mr Mould.

The only thing getting in the way was that, Mr Mould—as Terrence had just decided to christen him—had grown legs, and eyes, and a mouth.

And looked mightily pissed off to boot.

3

A LL THE AIR LEAKED from Terrence's lungs. His whole body was struck numb. And that burned rubber smell got all the more overwhelming. Now seemed to form a seal over his mouth and nostrils. And to choke him with all its might . . . did smells really have might?

He remembered that he'd taken off his glasses. He still had them clutched in his fist.

That was it.

Had to be it.

He whipped them up. Slipped them on over his nose.

Looked out.

Still there.

Mr Mould was still there.

He allowed his washing-up-gloved hands to drop down by his sides and felt the residue water sop into his jean pockets. It made him shudder. But not as much as when Mr Mould decided to use that newly formed mouth of his to speak.

"Wha' the hell ya playin' at, eh?"

Terrence just glowered back at him. At Mr Mould. Just *trying* to work out how he might respond to that comment.

Now that Terrence thought about it, Mr Mould looked a little like a crisp that had been soaked in a dish of water for a couple of days or so. Not that that accounted for the peachy colour.

And those legs.

Those eyes.

The mouth.

The legs seemed like they'd once been toothpicks, only they'd gone through some hideous—and perhaps nuclear—transformation to appear in the condition they did.

They looked all . . . well, *furry*. Hardly substantial enough to hold up the mass of Mr Mould. But the fact remained that they were.

The eyes and mouth, if that was what he could call them . . . well, the 'eyes' *were* looking dead at him, and that 'mouth' *had* just said something to him . . . they were just holes. No more than three marks that it seemed someone had made with the prongs of a fork.

Or by twizzling the tip of a knife blade.

"Well?" Mr Mould said, suddenly sprouting toothpick arms to go with those legs.

They looked just as equally unsubstantial, but they did the trick, allowing Mr Mould to, quite clearly, rest his hands on his hips— were those hips?

"Uh, uh, uh," Terrence said, backing away, his natural urge to flee taking over.

He had often speculated that that was the main reason his gene pool had got through all these years, because it certainly wasn't muscles, or attractiveness.

Or brain power, really, thinking about it.

Mr Mould took a step—that's right! A *step!*—across the base of the kitchen sink, hands still on his hips, and those gouged-out holes that appeared to serve as eyes still staring right at the bridge of Terrence's nose. "Speak, do you?" Mr Mould said.

This time Terrence couldn't even summon an 'uh,' and when he took another step back he came into contact with the tiled kitchen wall. For some reason he just stopped.

Didn't think to turn and run, to raise the alarm.

Perhaps somehow his subconscious got home to him about just how ridiculous it would be for him to rush about the house screaming about a rogue scrap of mould taking on life.

Bald Paul would most likely just think he was making excuses.

And that girl would pout at him.

Terrence waited. Staring. Waiting for Mr Mould to say something else.

Finally, he did.

Mr Mould slipped one of his 'hands' off his waist and reached back over his shoulder, took to scratching at the back of his neck. "Know how long I been here? Festering?"

Numbed, Terrence shook his head.

"Two months," Mr Mould said.

From the way he said it, the room he left for those words to echo, Terrence was certain that Mr Mould hoped the statement would shock him. But, in fact, it seemed just about right.

From upstairs, through what he often thought of as *precariously* thin floorboards, Terrence heard a girlish giggle. Bald Paul's bedroom was right above their heads. Right above the kitchen.

Mr Mould tilted his neck back and took a long look at the ceiling.

For some reason, it was now that Terrence found his voice. "That's my, uh, my housemate, up there."

Mr Mould continued to stare up at the ceiling. Apparently transfixed by that giggling. And the mumbling grumble that Terrence knew to recognise as Bald Paul's voice through walls.

Slowly, Mr Mould brought his head back down, angled his neck and looked to Terrence. "And what're you doing?"

"Uh, pardon?"

"What're you doing?"

"I'm, well, you know, I've got to clean, uh, clean out the sink."

Mr Mould treated this response with a steely glare, though Terrence wasn't all that sure just how it'd be possible for Mr Mould to perform anything *but* a steely glare.

He only had a pair of holes for eyes, after all.

"Stitched you up, did they?" Mr Mould said.

"What?"

"They tell you that *you* had to sort out the mould in the sink, sort *me* out, eh?"

Terrence thought back. To the drawing of straws. To those rainbow-streaked plastic straws they'd all slipped out of Bald Paul's bunched up fist. And he remembered looking to his three other housemates, all of them bearing hearty grins, before turning to look at Bald Paul—seeing that *he* had the heartiest grin of all.

Next up, Terrence had looked down to the straw he'd pulled.

Short. Half the length of the others.

And that was that.

And here he was.

Speaking with the mould.

Terrence turned his attention back to the mould, to Mr Mould . . . he supposed there wasn't much point in not being consistent with his nomenclature now that he'd somehow managed to tumble down the Crazy Hole, after getting whacked several times by every branch in the Crazy Tree, having fallen out of the Crazy Sky . . . etcetera, etcetera, etcetera.

And then, deep in the pit of his stomach, he felt a warmth. A spark. Then a kindling sensation. Like something was growing inside of him. Not mould—*no!*—it was much brighter than that. A pure, *positive* feeling. A feeling of confidence. Of inner strength.

And now he thought it the right time to turn his attention to Mr Mould. To ask him the question out straight, just how he'd seen it in films, asked over and over a million times before: by stable boys, and by mages' apprentices, and by lowly peasants even.

He took a deep breath, no longer caring about that burned rubber stench, that hint of manure there too, and he came right on out with it.

"Are you . . . are you going to show me how to, you know, how to stand up for myself? How to make something of myself?"

Mr Mould remained where he was. On those sturdy-yet-improbable toothpick legs of his. That pair of holes for eyes bore into him.

This time, it came down to Terrence to break the silence between them. "Well?" Terrence said. "Is that it? Is that what all this is about?"

Mr Mould's arms hung limply down at his sides now. And his gaze seemed to soften for the first time in their acquaintanceship, as if he had shifted away from that previous confrontational attitude of his, and then he said, "Mate, the only one that can help you now is a psychologist. You're talking to mould, for Christ's sake, go get professional help."

And, with that, Mr Mould slicked back in on himself.

Once more flattened down into a smudge of peach-coloured mould.

Nothing more, nothing less.

Terrence just stood, back still resting against the tiled wall of the kitchen, his mind throwing off sparks from all the thinking it was doing.

Approximately five minutes later, he shifted out of his daze, blinked it away, and then resumed his cleaning of the mould from the base of the kitchen sink.

Once he got through, he hung the washing-up gloves off the side of the sink, and then wandered off up to his bedroom, where he lay back on his bed for a long time, listening to the passionate grunts and girly giggles wade through the paper-thin walls.

And as he stared up at that eggshell coloured ceiling, long since discoloured by damp, and—inexplicably—a few shoe marks, he thought things through. Thought about the lab. And thought about just who he was as a person.

As a *man*.

And it was right then that he swore vengeance on his housemates. That *somehow* he would find a way to get even with them. He would find a way to get them back for them making him do everything round here, from that drawing of straws, making him clean out that sink, to all those times they'd steal his food from the cupboards and then lie right to his face.

Because he couldn't care less what the mould had told him.

He didn't need professional help.

What he needed, and it seemed totally clear to him now, was to grow a pair.

REQUIEM FOR A TELEPATH

H ISS. CLICK-CLICK. BEEP.
 Bop.
Hiss. Click-click. Beep.

Bop.

The problem with being a telepath is that you have no way of knowing when you're going to die.

Just not part and parcel of the ability.

That's what you learn fairly early on: the limits of your ability, because you do go out scouting the frontiers as much as you can. And those days are mostly ones of disappointment, it heavies my heart to say. Still, it can't be said that being a telepath is at all a minor thing. On the contrary, while you're alive, it's one of the greatest gifts ever given . . . a *sixth* sense, if you will.

It opens doors . . . hmm, no that's probably not quite the right way to put it—a better way might be to say that it shunts you right through doors, busts them right off their hinges.

Quite simply put, being a telepath is just about the greatest single ability any person can have.

Something that turns them into a superhuman.

And, I have to admit, that I didn't shirk my power whatsoever, that I was ready and willing to take on just about every advantage it would give me. I wanted to push it right out to the very edge of its limits, and then go on a little further.

I wanted to be nothing short of a super*man.*

I have a distinct memory of the exact moment when I discovered my ability. As I remember, it was a cold morning, snowing outside, and in our modest, middle-class home, a fire was blazing away in the wood-burning kitchen stove and my mother was chopping leek and potatoes to put into a soup we'd be having for lunch.

I must've been four years old, or so, since I hadn't yet started school.

Didn't even have a conception of what school might mean.

I remember just how cosy those days were, how full of warmth the house always was, and how there was this slight odour of wood smoke constantly about the place. Not at a level that would make you cough, let alone choke, but one that reminded me of charcoal, of that reassuring smell.

That morning I had hardly finished my artificially flavoured, raspberry cereal before my mother headed off to get cooking on lunch. I could still taste that sugary, manufactured raspberry flavour at the back of my mouth. It must've been a Saturday or a Sunday, with us all about to eat together, my father maybe out at the shops, or gluing his models out in the garage with his electric heater flipped up to maximum, a scarf draped about his neck.

As for myself, I was sitting on the floor playing with a wooden train of mine, one that I suppose I'd just got for Christmas, or maybe for my birthday—since my birthday is in January that time period has a habit of blending all together.

I remember being fascinated by the sound of the wooden train wheels against the laminate flooring of the kitchen, how it made this odd zipping sound as I whipped the train back and forth.

I sensed my mother glancing back at me several times, looking over her shoulder, a slight smile on her face, and her cheeks all flushed from the warmth of the wood-burning stove crackling away in the corner of the kitchen.

It was then that I heard it.

Heard the thought.

My *first* thought.

—*maybe just one*—

I remember tilting my little head upwards and gazing at my

mother, still at the stove, her back to me, and saying, "Why 'just one', Mummy?"

She ceased chopping. Her shoulders seized up. All the muscles on her neck went rigid, and I was sure that I could see the blood ticking through her veins.

When she turned to look at me, she had a faraway look in her eye, a slight look of concern. "What . . . what was that, baby?"

But, even at four years old, I knew that what I had asked had stirred emotions in my mother, and I knew that it was better for me just to say nothing, and so I shook my head and went back to playing with my train. To scooting it back and forth along the kitchen floor, making that cool zipping sound. And a little while later my mother returned to her chopping.

But I didn't forget what I had heard.

It was impossible.

From that time onwards, I knew that I was different.

That I was *superior* to the rest of them.

2

I T WASN'T TILL I started school, and had flushed my way through the first few years, that I fully began to gain a grasp on my power. To find some way of controlling it. Of *being able* to control.

I have to admit, though I made a good job of hiding it, I was tormented throughout the days with the voices from inside other people's minds. Hearing them constantly speak, and think.

All these words and phrases I'd never heard before.

Things a child had no business hearing.

And from my own mother and father *too*.

It must've been around the middle of the summer, and I might've been seven or eight by then, all I recall is that the nights had grown hot and humid and sticky, and I spent most of the time rolling about on my mattress, my sheet becoming a more and more screwed-up ball at the foot of my bed. Every hour or so I would have to get up and go to the kitchen, pour myself out a glass of water to take care of the parched sensation in my mouth. And I remember smelling the grass cuttings in those long, light summer nights, and hearing the lawnmowers starting up in the late evening just as I was going off to bed. And little me just lying there, staring up at the ceiling, blinking every so often, hearing every last thought of my mother and father as if they spoke to me from the distance from inside of an echo chamber.

At least then, at that age, I knew that I could escape the voices if only I could get myself far away.

Far enough away from everyone else.

Maybe it was around eleven in the evening, perhaps a little later —my parents were always late-to-bed, early-to-rise people. *Busy* people. No time for sleep. Maybe that's where I got my own work ethic from, on reflection.

I had just finished off my latest glass of water and I swung myself up and out of bed, made my way off along the hallway, making for the bathroom.

But I froze.

Something didn't feel right.

The bathroom door wasn't shut. But the door was only open a hair's breadth.

I knew there was someone inside.

My mother or father.

My heart lodged in my throat and I felt myself go all hot all over, and then cold.

And that was when the voice began. When I started to hear her thoughts.

—*nothing left . . . nothing left . . . nothing left*—

It was like a mantra.

Over and over again.

But it was the way it faded away slowly.

As if my mother was sinking down into a lake.

I clutched the empty glass tighter in my fist, took another few steps forward, and then reached out for the door. Gave it a little shove.

The door opened with an unoiled *creak*.

My mother lay on the floor. On her back. Arms and legs spread-eagled on the black-and-white bathroom tiles. Her eyes half open. Eyeballs lolling about their sockets.

I remember staring, for the longest time, at her chest as it rose and fell against her beige V-neck top, and then to a small damp patch just in the centre of her chest, in between her breasts. Only when I looked up to her face, saw the drool gathering—*pooling*—in the corner of her mouth, did I realise what it was. I turned my attention to the brown, translucent plastic bottle beside her. Totally empty. Its white cap upturned, discarded there too.

"Mummy?" I said, clutching that glass even tighter still.

But she couldn't hear me.

Not now.

She had gone away. Had managed to escape from me.

From us.

From me and my father.

I remember becoming intensely aware of the glass I grasped in my hand, and there was a voice in my brain telling me not to drop it. To make *absolutely sure* not to drop it.

That wasn't someone else's voice in *their* head.

It was the voice inside of *my* head.

And I knew, from then onwards, I would be able to keep myself separate from everyone else. That the key was just to remember how *I* sounded like. Not to try and block the other voices from getting in, but to keep my own apart.

That was the only way I would be able to save my sanity.

3

THOUGH I REMEMBER so many discussions back home, with my father on the phone to various people, hearing all those thoughts skittering through his brain, I did my best not to pay attention to them. To tune out. To take a pair of headphones and hook myself up to the stereo, and to listen to the CDs of classical music my father kept stuffed in bookcases.

To blare all the voices away.

In the end it was decided that my mother would come home.

Before my mother came home, me and my father converted the sitting room downstairs into my mother's bedroom. We bought her a wide, easy-access bed, and together we picked out some sleek, beautiful silk sheets, and took great care in finding an extremely comfortable armchair, where she would be able to sit and look out the window.

Out into our garden.

To the rose bushes, and to the twittering birds, and be able to breathe in all the nature.

She arrived home in an ambulance. It was like she had aged several decades. She needed a frame to walk around. And, even then, either me or my father would stand alongside her in case she became too frail and toppled over to one side or the other.

When she couldn't walk any longer, and we had to wheel her about in a chair, my job, whenever I came home from school, was to take her out, to take her down our street, along the asphalt pavement, and to the park at the end of the road. I'd wheel her around twice—around the gravel path, around the fountain that had long lost its pressure and now only squirted out a vague dribble . . . like that dribble I'd seen at the corner of my mother's mouth, while she lay on the bathroom floor. I would speak to her. Say reassuring things.

So I wouldn't have to listen to her thoughts.

To what she said, over and over again.

—*nothing left . . . nothing left . . . nothing left*—

It was only when we were alone, on those afternoons when I would get home from school, and right before I'd have to crack on with my homework, that I would go in to see her.

I would sit down on the edge of the mattress and speak to her.

Just *speak* to her.

And try to tune myself out of her thoughts.

Though, in reality, it was impossible.

Not at that age. Not with the level of my abilities.

It would take me much longer before I could properly understand the gift I had.

But—and it still shames me to admit it today—those were the occasions which I learned to take and use for my own education.

To better sharpen my gift.

To allow my mind to meld into my mother's, and to feast myself on her memories, on everything she had known. She put up no resistance.

I would sit on the edge of the mattress and I would lose myself in my mother's emerald-green eyes, lose myself in the sleek, shadow-white reflections that bounced across their surface. And I would burrow into her memories. Pluck them out. One by one. Examine them. Hold them up for scrutiny. And that is how I was able to experience, among other things, my birth.

Through my mother's eyes.

One afternoon, we were sitting there, neither of us speaking, me buried deep into my mother's mind, going through those scattered memories, leaving that constant, unstoppable, unchained thought . . .

—nothing left . . . nothing left . . . nothing left—

. . . behind, almost reduced to simple back chatter on a radio, a channel crossed over another, hardly more than a whisper now.

At that point I had learned how to switch up the volume of voices in the heads of others, and how to turn them down. Though not how to mute them completely. How to shut them out of my head when I wished for privacy.

It was my mother who brought me around, brought me away from my perusing of her memories. Her head jerked quickly to the side. And her eyes went all matted. All the life seemed to slink from them. When I followed her gaze, I saw my father standing in the doorway, staring at us. Or, more specifically, staring at *me*.

He had the wide-brimmed straw hat he always wore in the summer, and his light-brown suit on. His cheeks were hollowed out, as they had become over the weeks that my mother had returned to live with us. His face was thick with stubble he hadn't bothered to shave away. I had also noticed a few streaks of grey in the back patches of his otherwise sable hair, though I hadn't so much as entertained the thought of telling him.

He clutched his leather briefcase—brown so it matched his suit —and I saw that his knuckles had turned white from lack of circulation, he was gripping the handle so tightly.

Neither of us said anything. He just kept on staring.

Right at me.

Though I listened hard to his thoughts, channelled myself into his mind, I could hear nothing.

Nothing at all.

I could smell him, though. That musky smell of body odour I've always associated with *hard work*. I could hear the gentle *click* of the phlegm at the back of his throat as he breathed in and out. My mouth just tasted stale, and felt dried up. I wanted to excuse myself to go and get a drink of water from the kitchen, but I knew that neither of us could speak.

Neither one of us could break this perfect frozen moment.

Though I didn't notice it till I felt a sharp, hammering pain flush up my arm, I realised that I'd been picking at a hangnail. That I had torn it loose. Blood was welling up in the wound, shining dully in the fading afternoon light. The smell wafting up and thickening in my nostrils.

And then, just like that, he was gone.

He said nothing.

My mother said nothing.

And, after I heard the back door slap shut, my father going out to the garage—back to his models till he got round to heating up our dinner—I turned my mind back to my mother's.

To listening to her thoughts.

To reading . . . no, *living* her memories.

4

T HINGS WENT ON more or less as normal, at home and at
school.

Of course I excelled in all my subjects, at least the ones that
required definite answers: maths, the sciences, among other things.
But I made no show of my flush of A grades because the arts
subjects were another matter. Though for some—history and, to a
degree, religious studies—I could meld myself into my teachers'
thoughts and extract the essence, the *basis*, of an answer, I could
never figure out English literature.

To begin with, I tried to second guess my teacher, to try and
delve deep into her memories, into her thoughts and feelings, and
to attempt to extrapolate just what it was she wanted us to put
down on the page. Oh, I always got the gist of it—the *thrust* of
whatever the essay or argument was supposed to be about—but
never anything better than a B.

And some damning praise.

I didn't let it worry me, though, and it wasn't like my mother or
father cared anyway.

Both of them lived in separate worlds now, far away from
my own.

Totally removed from my own.

They had little way of knowing just how intimately I knew
about their own lives, their own memories, their deeply guarded
hopes and dreams. Things that they might not have realised themselves on a conscious level. But some things aren't meant to be
shared.

Some things should just be kept behind sealed lips.

It was in one of my English classes where I set eyes on Philippa.

All told, I must've been about fifteen, maybe even sixteen, on the verge of finishing school, and leaving all this *education* behind.

She made one of those most difficult of moves, arriving to our school in the penultimate—*or was it the ultimate?*—year before graduation.

I remember her wandering into our English class one frosty winter's morning, filing along in her freshly bought school uniform —an odd sludge-green shade—her hemp-woven messenger bag bucking against her lower back. She smelled kind of like peaches, though that might sound just a little cliché. But that was how she smelled. Her hair was blond, and her features delicate, and her eyes a soft blue shade. I can still recall the exact sound as she sat down. It was almost inaudible, just a slight scuff of the chair legs against the classroom carpet. A slight *thump* as she dropped her bag down at her feet.

But it was what everyone else couldn't hear.

What I *could* hear.

That was what made all the difference.

—*here we go again*—

And when I saw her blow out her cheeks with a hefty sigh, I couldn't help but give a small giggle to myself. Almost under my breath. Loud enough for *her* to hear, though.

Have her stare right at me.

Those crystalline eyes meeting mine for the first time.

And I must've still been smiling, because, soon enough, she smiled right back at me.

And I felt a warmth rise in my chest. Almost as if my heart had sunk into my stomach. I could feel the throb of my pulse in my mouth. At the base of my tongue.

Soon after, our teacher wandered in through the door, and I turned back to the front, like a Good Little Boy. Unbeknownst to my teacher, I was still working on cracking into her deepest level of thoughts, wherever it was that she kept all those answers—all those *things*—she wanted to see in our essays. I was determined to get to it eventually.

To get something higher than a B.

But, that day, I scrounged next to nothing. I simply couldn't focus enough on the problem, couldn't get any leverage on her brain at all.

And I felt her memories slipping through my fingers like so many bars of soap.

Because Philippa was on my mind.

Totally and completely occupying it.

As she would for many years to come.

5

ONE OF THE GREAT THINGS about my gift is the ability to see through people's words, and to see right through to their very innermost thoughts. To skim past the subtexts, and dive right down to the point. And to use it for my own ends, more often than not.

For the longest time, ever since I first asked Philippa to that film, asked her out on a *date*, I had made her my own private project. I had instructed myself on how to learn to know her. To grasp with those different levels, those things that she said inside of her mind, and not out of her mouth.

She was my guinea pig.

Albeit an extremely attractive one.

I could tell when she was bored, when her attention was receding from me, and I would *always* act on it, come up with something witty, or do something odd to take her mind off it. And I would get a double hit. See that pearly white smile of hers blended with that leaky, osmosis effect of sharing the warmth that passed through her as she laughed.

I could sense her annoyances—mostly towards her parents— and I would make subtle comments, ask just the right question, get her to look at me with those wide eyes of hers . . . and, more than once, hear her say, "It's like you can read my mind, you know?"

So maybe it was inevitable that one day we would reach an impasse, of sorts.

It was after I'd taken her to visit my mother for the first time, and she'd seen us together, seen me delving into her memories . . . I couldn't help it, it was worse than a drug addiction, it was more of a conditioned habit, a reflex, even, just completely impossible to refrain from doing, no matter who was there with me. While I was pretty certain Philippa couldn't see just what I was doing, she did confront me out in the hall, after we'd been in there with my mother. After we had helped her into bed, pulled the blankets up to her chin the way she liked, and left her there, lying on her back and staring at the ceiling. Philippa took hold of my hand with her soft fingers, and I smelled her peachy scent waft over me. I could almost taste those peach segments. And then she said, in a lowered voice, "It's funny, you know?"

"What?"

"Well, it's like how sometimes you're reading my mind. Like you can tell exactly what it is that I've got going on, you know?"

I'm sure that I flushed just a little, though the lighting out in the hallway was fairly dim, so I doubt she noticed. I waited for her to finish. Not wanting to reveal myself unless I had to.

Unless it became totally inevitable.

"Sometimes I feel like, uh . . ." She stopped, smiled and looked away.

"What?" I said. "You can tell me. You can tell me anything, you know?"

She smirked a little, and gave her head a little shake, and then, when she looked back into my eyes, said, "Nah, it's stupid. Don't worry about it. Really. It's just . . . just a weird thing, that's all."

"Really? You can tell me if you want."

Again, she shook her head, squeezed my hand a little tighter, and then her smile slipped from her lips. She was looking out, over my shoulder.

When I turned around, I saw my father was standing in the kitchen doorway, that he was glowering at the two of us . . . just like a slighted father should look.

I was sure he would say something then.

That he would give me away.

But, like before, he said nothing.

And, a few moments later, he left us in peace.

6

I T CAME ABOUT soon enough—the end of how things had been.

How I'd been living with my parents.

I announced my ambition to my father, that I no longer wanted to continue my education, that I wanted to try my luck out in the Big Bad World. Out in the city.

He was a little disappointed.

I could tell.

He had always been an academic soul. Always reading. Studying. But, above all else, constantly fiddling with his models. Out in that garage, where no one could get to him.

Where he *thought* no one could get to him.

After long, heart-wrought discussions, we decided that the best plan of action, what with me leaving home—*hopefully for good*—was for my mother to leave and go to a care home.

For her to be taken care of by professionals.

My father and me decided that once we'd got enough saved between the two of us—once we'd got enough coming in between the two of us—we would bring my mother home and hire a personal carer. But that was some way off yet.

I coasted through school for the final few weeks, doing the best I could with the tests, and striking it lucky in one of my chemistry exams, having one of the invigilators completing the papers we were sitting, 'for *fun*', I suppose. Little did he know that he slipped me the answers.

Every last one.

It was at the School Leavers' Ball when the culmination of my practice on Philippa reached its zenith. And I heard her soul borne out in her mind's eye.

Well, if truth be told, I *brought* it into her mind's eye.

Just gave it a little, playful prod that's all.

—if you asked me to marry you right now I would say yes . . . all you have to do is ask—

I looked to her. To the feathered, jasmine-coloured dress she wore, and looked to her floaty blond hair, and to her lightly brushed-on eye shadow. And I wondered, if I hadn't had my gift at all, whether I might be able to divine just what it was she wanted.

If I *really* knew her as well as she believed I did.

But, right then and there, I decided that it wasn't worth thinking about. That there was no point in speculating about *what if's* and *how might's*, there was only the present.

Only now.

So I popped the question.

And she accepted.

Though we had no money, and the blessing of neither sets of our parents, we strode on out of our pokey little town and headed for the city. I had my apprenticeship at one of the big financial firms, and she had aspirations for being a singer . . . though I had long ago sifted through her innermost subconscious and determined that, really—*really*—that wasn't where her passion lay. That whereas she believed she was at home in smoky clubs, practising her heart out on half-drunk executives and their receptionist lovers, I knew that what she really wanted was to paint.

To pick out a nice, quiet spot.

And to throw paint at a canvas.

But, I decided, some things were precious. Important to find out for oneself.

Though I *would* lock it away for later.

For when I needed a line of credit.

Needed a sturdy tool to make up for something.

A great, honking sledgehammer.

7

THOUGH WE KEPT quite separate schedules—me to the nine-to-five grind, and Philippa to the late nights and early mornings—we still remained thoroughly entwined in each other's lives despite the passing years. I would yank off my tie, screw it up and bury it deep down into one of the pockets of my suit, and go off to whichever club she happened to be playing that evening.

I'd sit over in a corner, out of her natural line of sight. And I would nurse a whisky, feeling its warmth flooding through my chest. I would smile to myself out of those shadows, think about how many minds I had read that day. How many *in's* I had managed to forge with various high-ranking members of the company. How I had just manage to stumble across *exactly* what it was they were looking for. Just *stumbled* right across it.

It wasn't long before I ploughed my way upwards, through the hierarchy of the firm, found myself almost being yanked between various executives, wanted for my stunning negotiating skills, and my calm, unerring patience.

I always seemed to do just the right thing.

To *know* just the right thing to say.

If only they'd known how I really did it.

That it was something that could never be taught to anybody.

And I'd never even want to try at all.

The impasse, the one with Philippa, came before I expected it. In all honesty, I suppose it arrived after a long two-year slog—the two of us sharing that tiny, broom cupboard of an apartment, and me just wanting to come home to fall into bed.

Not having the energy—*or patience*—for her singing any longer.

Knowing that it wasn't worthwhile chasing a dream that could never be.

That the holder never *really* wanted to achieve.

The exact moment cropped up just after I'd returned from a weekend-long business trip, and some drunk had tossed a pint of beer right over her.

Though she was no stranger to hecklers, to drunks, her despondency was due to something she'd heard on leaving the club. From one of the bouncers. How he'd said to his friend—*equally bald and meat-headed*—how Philippa was one of those 'no-hopers'.

The ones they saw every night of the week.

But could never see themselves for who they truly were.

Well, I spent a long time consoling her. My arm round her shoulder. Her crying into my shirt. Me feeling her tremble, as if this realisation was having some deeper physiological effect on her. I stayed out of her mind. Gave her privacy. Because I already knew just where she was headed.

What her *true* ambition in life was.

And soon she would see it for herself.

At last, she saw sense, deciding to throw in the towel with the singing, no longer to go out to the clubs and stand up there for the ridicule of drunks.

I'm not sure what moved me, it might've been just seeing her at home, all huddled up on the sofa, watching TV all day, a tissue crushed in one fist, and the other gripping tight to the hem of the blanket draped over her. I remember how glazed over her eyes were —how I almost imagined seeing the TV light shining back off her eyes.

Or maybe I'm being nostalgic.

More likely, though, it was the day that I came back home, a few years into our marriage—us being around our mid-twenties by then—and I caught her looking at me in that way; that way that meant I had no need to read her thoughts at all.

Not at that time, in any case.
I knew just what she wanted to say.
She wanted a baby.
Of course she did.
Something to take her mind off things.

8

I SHUFFLED UP the still-warm blanket and made myself some space beside her on the sofa. I embraced her, like I always seemed to be doing in those days, and I felt how frail she was, how her bones were just like a bird's bones . . . *that* fragile. And I could sense her mind ebbing and lapping, like a tide, unfocussed and unhinged with no direction.

Desperately needing direction.

Of course, at that point, there would've been no problem in us having a baby together. As far as things had gone on, I was already far ahead at work. Earning money that most employees couldn't dream of before they'd served ten years, and I was working on edging my way in as the boss's Golden Boy.

I outlined things as clearly as I could, as logically, as clear-headedly as I could, but it was tricky, really tricky to reason with her, to make her see past the obvious, to make her see that it wasn't a matter of her being talent*less* but more a matter of her not having found her true vocation.

I had to help her.

There was no other way.

So, one day, on the way back from work, I drifted on into the apartment with some paint, a canvas, some brushes. I caught Philippa on the sofa, in that same posture of hers. TV flickering away. Washing the sitting room in its luminescent glow. I remember the clear way her head turned to me, and how her gaze dropped—dropped down to what I held in my hand, down by my side. And then, as she raised her head upwards again, to meet my eye, I saw it.

Saw the *glimmer* there.

That was just what it was.

Like something deep inside of her had sparked.

Had been relit and set kindling by the mere sight of these pieces of equipment.

I felt my heart flutter. Felt my cheeks go all hot—then all cold. And I could suddenly smell those dry odours of the paint, even though the paint itself was well-sealed within the tins, and within the plastic bags. I could almost *taste* the paint on my tongue.

Like blood . . . but more neutral, more *manufactured*.

I'm not certain just what I expected—for her to chuck off the blanket from the sofa, for her to run into my arms, and to smother me with kisses and hugs, and thank yous.

Perhaps, if she'd truly understood herself, she might've done that.

But she still had a way to go.

A way to go before she *fully* understood the matter.

9

AT FIRST I WAS DISAPPOINTED, I have to admit. I somehow half-expected to come home from the next day after work and to find all those canvases covered in paint, and my wife—*Philippa*—grinning, wearing those overalls I had picked out at that same shop, herself also covered in paint. But she was still in the same place.

On the sofa.

TV switched on.

Light washing over her.

I felt angry at first, and then told myself to calm down, told myself that it was my gift—that my gift set me apart from the rest of the world . . . made me *super*human. I could not rely on mere mortals to march the world at my pace. I suppose, for them, I was something of a blur.

I continued to come home, expecting every day. And I would find her there. Still watching TV. Glued to the set. The painting equipment untouched.

It was around that time when I was promoted to be the boss's right-hand man. I was to go where he went. I was to always be at his beck and call—to be the one that he could depend on.

But, above all else, I was always to be at the table when it came to negotiations.

Just as he always had the greatest of pleasure declaring, *I* had never been involved in a negotiation that I hadn't come out of as the winner.

It was as part of this new role, however, that I found myself called away from home, called to accompany my boss on a trip abroad—on the company jet.

At first I was a little apprehensive about leaving Philippa

behind. I worked out a way to plant an idea in the boss's head that she should be brought along. But my boss's mind was thick. And it was hard to penetrate. Like stepping into a gloomy forest and expecting to find and trap a rabbit.

Not that I wasn't working on it.

Working on *him*.

Did I think she was suicidal?

. . . No, I don't think so. After all, I had experienced those emotions up close—what with my mother and the bathroom floor, and those pills. I *knew* just how that felt.

No, it was . . . well, a little more subtle. A little more dulled, yet still glimmering.

There was a spark of hope somewhere within Philippa's id, and I had spotted it, noticed it there like a pearl lying in a the thick grass of a night-time lawn. And I knew, so long as that pearl continued to gleam, that Philippa would not leave me behind, that she wouldn't do something that would plague the rest of my life.

Ruin the rest of my life.

And so I left. Went with my boss to the meeting.

10

TWO, THREE DAYS LATER, I returned to our apartment, and I remember feeling that sticky sensation in my throat, as if something was lodged there, as if I had a cold coming on.

At the time I subconsciously blamed it on the effects of having been constrained by cabin pressure for hours on end. Later, I learned to recognise that sensation for what it was:

A premonition.

As I swung open the thick oak door into our apartment, my eyes immediately fell onto the sofa before me. Onto the TV.

It was switched off.

The sofa was vacant.

And Philippa was nowhere in sight.

Already, I found myself swearing inside my mind, and I recall dropping my luggage with a deep *thud* at the door and rushing to the kitchen.

Seeing she wasn't there, I kept on going:

To the sitting room.

To the bathroom.

And then, finally, when I had almost given up hope altogether, thought that she might've taken the chance to skip out—to leave me alone—I heard the shuffling slide of the French Doors that led out onto the patio. That slightly dejected little spot. A rectangular space between exterior walls of the apartment. Populated entirely by concrete slabs and dying plants.

I listened for the door to slide back into place. And then for Philippa, dressed in those paint-splatted overalls, and grinning at me, some of the paint clumped in her blond hair, to emerge from the shade of the patio and into the light glow of the house.

It was like a dream coming true.
Even to this day I can hardly believe it.

A T WORK, things moved faster still.

I shot up, through various promotions till I was in a real position of power—until I myself had some stake in the company, and my boss had taken to calling me his own son, or terms like it.

I knew I had set myself up for life.

Me and Philippa had kids; three of them: two boys and a girl, I allowed her to name them all, and I was keen to ensure that she nurtured her own talents while bringing them up.

So we hired a nanny, and she got on with her painting.

Around that time, I received a call from my father.

The first for many years.

We had hardly spoken at all since my mother had gone to the care home—what did we have to talk about?

It was good timing, in retrospect. In fact, I want to claim that I was thinking of calling him myself . . . but I had simply not ever got around to it. Really, the fact was that I was afraid. I thought about how he had looked at me. Of how he knew just what I was—or that he at least had an inkling.

Speaking on the phone has always made me uneasy.

I have no chance of reading the mind of the caller.

All I can hear is their voice, and none of those accompanying notes, none of the subtle tones that go on between the ears but never come out through the lips.

So perhaps it was a good thing that my father had little to say. Or, at least, there was very little to be read between the lines of the words he spoke:

My mother was dead.

I HAD OFTEN thought about the day. About how I might feel. How I would most likely just double over myself, lock the bathroom door and cry all my emotion out.

But I did the opposite.

My heart turned stone, and a deathlike chill descended.

Because I knew the truth. That I had so many memories of my mother's all stacked inside of my head. And that—in a much more literal way than people say it—she would always be with me.

Her body was gone. Her mind too.

But her memories remained within my brain.

We packed up our house in the city—the one we had bought after the second child—and we headed back out to the town where both our parents lived. Back to everything we had left behind.

The service was simple, but elegant. My father kept himself as wrapped up as I had known him to do throughout his life—why would *that* be any different now? And then, after everything was said and done, me and Philippa headed to the refreshments and watched our children run about, bobbing in and out from beneath the white tablecloths, chasing one another.

I remember looking up to see my father staring. To see him holding a glass of white wine in his pasty fist, and his black eyes just gazing out into space. And it was then that our oldest—Thomas—came up to me, pulled on the leg of my trousers, and asked, "Daddy, who's that man?"

When I told him the truth, that *that man* was in fact his grandfather, he just looked all vague, glanced back at my father, and then headed back off to play with the other two children.

Apparently unfazed that I had neglected to introduce him to his previous generation his whole entire life. What did it matter to him?

. . . And it wasn't like my father had extended himself towards us, either.

On the contrary, he had just slunk back into the shadows, retreated into himself as much as my mother had done. At least what had happened to her had been diagnosed, had been treated like an *illness*. For my father, though, that had never happened.

It was when we were rounding up the children, on our way back across the gravel car park when I sensed those thoughts. The thoughts of my father ebbing about at the fringes of my mind.

Sure enough, when I turned around, there he was, looking shabby in his black jacket and black tie, one of his shoes untied.

I told Philippa and the kids to get in the car and then slowly made my way over to him. To speak with him. I remember how his eyes had looked all mushy, all watery, as if he had been crying long and hard . . .

I thought he might be about to crack at any moment. That the flawless, straight-faced façade he had put up all these years might be about to split right open in spectacular fashion.

Wasn't this, after all, the day that his wife had died?

But all he did was eye me.

And I continued to drink in his vacant thoughts.

Hardly able to hold onto anything tangible.

In the end I gave up—I just retreated away from *his* mind.

When he spoke, he took me off guard. More because his voice was so rich and sure. "You aren't like me, are you, son?"

I swallowed hard. Looked back to the car. Saw the kids in the back, squabbling between themselves, and then I saw Philippa, sitting in the front seat, gazing out from beneath the windscreen. Looking concerned.

I looked to his face, took in those dried-up, cracked lips of his. "I . . . I don't know what you mean."

He gave me the vaguest outline of a smile, patted me on the shoulder. As he slunk away, he said, "Take care, son."

I NEVER SAW my father again before his death a year or so later.

Though the doctors might've said different, I'm certain what killed him.

That he saw nothing.

No *hope* left.

All his candles had gone out.

Even his own son had abandoned him . . . or whatever had taken *hold* of his son had carried away the boy he had fathered—the boy he had once known.

I took things slowly after hearing of his death, but had no intention of missing so much as a day of work. I knew that I had to keep up my position—go through with the enormous amount of responsibility that weighed down on my shoulders.

My role in the company.

I would be taking things over—incurring the wrath of my boss's son, and the self-appointed heir.

He had never bargained on a telepath, on someone more talented than he was, butting in and stealing his glory.

Sticking a knife through the belly of his birthright.

THE YEARS WENT BY for me—just like any other mortal —and I watched my children grow older, studied them, of course, for any signs of my own abilities, but saw nothing.

Nothing at all.

They all had the blue eyes of their mother, so it shouldn't have been a surprise, and, in a way, I was glad.

Why, they would have a good enough inheritance with what material wealth and influence I was leaving behind without having metaphysical gifts to boot. And it was partially for that reason that me and Philippa decided to sell the house in the city once the last of the kids had flown the nest, and go and take up in the countryside.

At work, things were ticking along just fine and I really had little day-to-day involvement there any longer. I trusted the good people to do what they did best. Whenever an important client came to town, I was always sure to head back to the office, to put on the personal touch, and to ensure that no mistakes were made.

To ensure that whoever it was we were doing business with was on the level.

Amongst other things.

And that leaves not a lot left to tell, only to say, that like all the mortals around me, I grew grey of hair and stout of belly. I took over the whole business once my boss died, and stepped up to the mantle, turned it in the direction I saw fit, right up till the moment of my retirement when I—gracefully—handed the reins over to the boss's son, let him take over the big calls for the last few years of *his* working life. Only months later, he had a heart attack.

I suppose some people don't have the belly of steel that business demands.

Me and Philippa retreated to our country home where we took long walks, and spent our nights beside the fire. Philippa's paintings adorned the walls . . . the ones that she hadn't *sold*, of course, for sizeable chunks of money. Money enough to rival, perhaps even surpass, my own business success.

We never did compare ledgers—get down to seeing just who was the breadwinner of the house—and I'm glad that we never did.

15

H ISS. CLICK-CLICK. BEEP.
      Bop.

Hiss. Click-click. Beep.

Bop.

I can hear the machines again, because that's what they are, aren't they?

Those fake sounds in my ears, though my brain should be elsewhere.

But my ability has not left me.

Not yet, anyway. Not while my heart is still beating.

You haven't left me either.

That is commendable.

If I were in your shoes then I might well have run for the door-way, gone to the crazy wing, or wherever they lock up the nutcases in these hospitals before sending them off some place with cushioned walls and suspicious-tasting food.

But you've stayed.

Good.

I can tell you're a good person . . . but do not worry, I really didn't delve *too* deep into your mind.

Didn't go right down into the depths of it.

But I have gone far enough to know you are good. I shall leave it at that.

I can also observe, from a distance, the details of my condition, of how I've ended up here, in this hospital bed, with these bleeping machines, though I really have no interest in knowing everything involved. I believe that at least *something* in my life should remain a mystery . . . and death seems as likely a fellow as any other.

Do, please, arrange for one thing, though. Now that you know my secret.

Just a minor thing really.

At my funeral, have them play a requiem.

A requiem for a telepath.

A PINT OF SUP

C OME ON IN YOUNG 'UN, that's it just draw up a stool, don't mind my ragged cloak or my rotten walking stick leaning up at the bar. My mangy dog Hella here's not been known to bite for many a year. You just take a seat right there and listen to me. What ya drinking? That so? Make it two—one for me, one for you. You'll be paying, wontcha? Gotta help an old, penniless man out when you can, eh? There was a time when the youngsters respected their old folk, not now though. Oh boy, those were the days. Long past. Now if an elderly man wants respect he has to come right out and demand it. How's that strike ya? Yeah, well, I thought as much, not interested in a word, just like I said.

That's it, darling, put the sup down right there. My arms ain't too strong but these lips have still got some suck to them! This sup's pretty creamy, but it's the best in town. I should know considering that I've spent the past few decades probing here and there, getting my tongue wet in whatever place. Eh? A story? Can't an old man drink his sup in peace any longer? Just have a little time to himself to stew over his sup? Nah, didn't think so. Not now. Not these days. All right, then, young 'un, suppose you'll get your way. Sure as hell I have a few stories up my sleeve that I could roll out for ya, that's if you're willing to listen? They all say they'll listen but they drift away, get distracted by the end, and I have to start right from the beginning—sometimes I just don't bother. But if you're sure you've got your listening ears on then I'll regale ya.

Twas a dark and lonely night—ha! it always seems like my tales start that way—and dawn was long in coming. Indeed some were bothered that it might not come at all, which is to say there was some whispering that there was evil afoot, and not that fairy-tale kind I'm sure you've heard about. This was the real deal, ancient and unmovable, rotten to the core. Hey! You listening to me or what? I can just as easily slink off to yonder corner with my sup and wait out this evening in peace. You sure. Well, all right. Then I'll go on.

As I said twas a thoroughly evil night. An artic gust writhed through the leaves and rain spurted down in equal parts ice and water, chilling all those that dared venture out from their houses and go forth into the streets. And those with any sense about them stayed in their houses, which is what cannot be said for the hero of our story, George Strangeblood. What d'ya mean that can't be his name? Of course it is. Why would I tell it if it wasn't? Kids nowadays don't know when to listen. Think they know it all. Just button your lip and hold your questions till afterwards, yeah? And don't think those answers are coming cheap, like, not without a good, old sup I don't answer questions.

George Strangeblood he was, and I challenge anyone to prove me otherwise. Problem was our George would've just liked to have stayed at home, had a sick daughter, see? In fact, as I understand it, she'd been in bed for several weeks—doctor's orders you might call it. Thing was where George lived was in the village of Port Nortle, that's the one that's leading right out into the Crimson Sea. Never heard of the Crimson Sea? Well, fancy that. Another thing you don't know. Who'd have thought it? Now how's about shutting up for good this time? Had your say? Good.

Anyway, thing was, with Port Nortle, was that it was nestled just into the coastline, swept up into the hillside just high enough to be out of reach of the crashing waves and just far enough below Death's Mountain, which towered above like some perched vulture ready to strike. The village was simple, a few dozen houses, no more—and certainly no doctor about the place. Whenever anyone needed much of anything—including doctors—they had to get it in through the port, that was unless they wanted to scale Death's

Mountain and cross over into Gotsome Town on the other side. I never much understood what made people live in Port Nortle, but there it was. People live in the strangest places, that's another slice of wisdom, you're getting your sup's worth, eh, young fellow?

Like I said, our friend here, George Strangeblood, he was getting all concerned like about his little girl. Oh her forehead was clammy and blue, all at the same time, and she was vomiting up whatever it was they got down her. She had started to tremoring whenever anyone got close, as if some kind of spectre hung round them. I'll tell you for nothing, young 'un, that spectre was nothing less than Death himself, he was there, ready to step in at a moment's notice—ready to be called upon.

So our George took it upon himself to make haste out of his home, and to stride forth through Port Nortle and scale the heights of Death's Mountain, so that he might save his little girl. As he left his house behind, there was a real quiver in the air, and it was a warning and I'll tell you what it was saying, it was saying, "Turn back George Strangeblood. Go back to your home and be beside your fire. Stay with your family or Death shall take two of you tonight." But George, being something of a stubborn fellow, refused to bend to the whim of the wind and so he wrapped his lambskin jacket round himself more tightly and marched along the water-front, past the thrashing waves and salty foam fluttering through the air, his eyes set only on one thing, and that was the path up Death's Mountain.

When he reached the first step that was when nerves took him whole. Oh they shook him up good, seizing hold of first his ankles and then working up to his thighs and, finally, his chest, where they froze his heart. His whole body became like a block of ice and wind skimmed his cheeks, robbing them of his cold sweats to boot. A full moon bobbed between clouds, taking mercy on the damned earth down below every once in a while, dabbing it with its effervescent glow. George gazed down at Port Nortle, to the houses crouched round the seafront in a jagged horseshoe, all of them looking out into the Crimson Sea, as if in expectation of the ship that would never come—not on a night such as this. He picked out his own house, the fourth from the edge of the village, and saw the glowing orange candlelight coming from his little girl's room and, I'm willing to wager, that spurred him right on, because from that moment forth he set about clambering up the rugged path leading up Death's Mountain.

Soon enough the rains blazed down upon him, soaking though his jacket and making his underwear cling to his skin. The wind would follow up—like a troublesome companion—chilling him right to the bone. When he glanced over his shoulder he fancied that he saw the spectre following after him, and he thought it right to be Death—you remember from before don't ya?—and he thought it good that Death would be occupied with him instead of his little girl. And so, through his misery and discomfort, he hefted himself up the steepening slope keeping himself parted from his ghastly stalker.

George Strangeblood got a good hundred or so feet up before he dared look back on Port Nortle again, back to those cosy houses, which looked cosier with each step. And then he glanced upward into the darkening sky, to where the peak of Death's Mountain peered down on him, daring him to continue his doomed journey.

Being that the villagers of Port Nortle would use boats to leave, and that the residents of Gotsome would use boats to round the coastline to sell their wares, the mountain path had become ill-maintained. The path itself had been so eroded by the hefty rains and looping winds that it was no wider than to allow a single man to pass along it. And with all the rain which fell on George Strange-blood, it meant that the remaining miniscule track was reduced to sloppy mud which squelched beneath foot and clung on with each step, and in general was not to be trusted to any great weight. Nonetheless, George Strangeblood kept going, slipping and near enough falling right off the face of Death's Mountain, till he had got himself three quarters up. And that was when he made the mistake of looking back.

Of course that was where Death lurked, ever present, just waiting his opportunity to give George that little shove, to let his frail human body barrel roll down the side of the mountain, breaking every bone as it went, before slapping it into a mound of mud and leaving it to be discovered the following summer when the frozen ground thawed.

"Where do you think you're going?" Death said, over the sound of the gales.

George Strangeblood hunched his shoulders in the heaving rain and squinted through the darkness. The moon peeked out from behind its cloud, giving him a better view of his pursuer. "To help my daughter," George Strangeblood said.

"It's an awful road," Death replied. "You'd be better off coming down, with me. Come let's walk back along this track, return to Port Nortle where you'll be safe."

"If I don't make it over the mountain then sure as anything my little girl shall die."

"That may be," Death said. "But there might well be two souls I take away this night if you do not come to your senses."

And I think you'll rightly recall that I mentioned such a thing. However, George Strangeblood remained unconvinced and he peered upward to the peak of Death's Mountain now so near. He had to shout over the wind to make himself heard. "Might I make a deal with you?"

"A deal with Death?" Death replied.

"If I am to make it over the mountain and into the town on the other side, you shall spare the life of my daughter, and keep your cold lips from hers until I return to her side. But, if I fail, then you may take both our lives, and carry us both off into the afterlife."

The hood of Death's sable cloak covered his face. He made no sound either of agreement or dispute, and George decided he must take this as a sign to continue on his quest—for if he was to meander any longer on this precarious ridge he would surely collapse from exhaustion and tumble into the valley below.

And where do you think you're going, young 'un? Oh, I see, off to buy an old man another pint of sup? Can't say I can fault your manners. Why, yes, that would do perfectly, and a bowl of water for my dog Hella, a leg of lamb to chew on. If he had any teeth to smile I'm sure he would. And if he weren't deaf as a post he might give you a bark of thanks, but as it is he prefers to say nothing lest he might agree to something he would regret.

Yes, there's only one way to drink sup and that's one after another. *Ha!* that's right, nothing that's worth learning can't get learnt from an old man, you'd be best served to teach yourself that lesson sharpish. I'll leave the other half for when I finish. If I drink it all now I might get myself confused and muddle up the whole thing.

Ah yes, I remember.

Our hero George he was striding and slipping all over the place. You see, as he got further and further up Death's Mountain he found it getting steeper and steeper, as if someone were tugging out the mountain from beneath his feet. He felt the presence of Death on his heels, and their ably struck deal hanging about him. It seemed that, with every step he took, the rain would hammer down harder or the wind would gust in stronger. He told himself that it was just his mind, thinking things over too hard, but he couldn't hardly forget it.

A gnawed-up signpost ahead announced the peak of Death's Mountain and he saw it before him, jutting out of the rock face like a single rotten tooth, ripe for plucking. He kept well away from the edge and stood lightly, afraid that at any moment something would betray him. His senses were stripped by now. Only the echoing howl of the wind sounded in his ears. He could still sense Death lingering on his heels, and how he wished he would go, but how he wished he would stay, so that his daughter might be saved a morbid fate. Doubled over, George looked over the peak and down into the darkened bowels of Port Nortle and then to the other side, where Gotsome Town spread itself below—streetlamps glimmering, swaying in the evening wind, and the sounds of merrymaking drifting upward on the mountain air. Oh how he wished to tell them of how life was like in Port Nortle, how it was they who held back the elements, laid into the other side of Death's Mountain, keeping Gotsome sheltered from storms such as this. His whole family, as far as it could be traced, had lived in Port Nortle and so, until tonight, he had seen no reason to change. But if he could only stave off death a mighty second longer, bring his daughter the much-needed medicine she required then he would leave forever.

Never to return.

Death sidled up beside George and said, "It's a tricky downward path, I'd say. If I were you I would turn back, go back the other way now you've come this far. Don't forget that if you do make it down it'll only be to come back up, and then you can be sure that your luck shan't hold."

George's teeth chattered together and his heart throbbed against his ribs. He stared down at the glowing warmth of Gotsome below and replied, "If I can find a doctor, get the medicine my daughter needs, then I shall be prepared to cross Death's Mountain another ten times, and dance on the peak my last time over."

Well, needless to say, Death didn't much like this bout of frivolity and so he sent George tumbling, down the mountainside with a single, sharp prod of his bony finger.

And George did tumble.

Just give me a break, won't you, young 'un? Let an old man wet his whiskers just a while. All this talk makes a man thirsty, don't you know? There, that's a good sup. Best in town and I should know. That's it, I leave the slops in the bottom of the glass for later on. All the goodness is in those bits. Best saved for last.

And so with George Strangeblood, he did tumble through soaking bracken. He knocked his knees and elbows on knobbly rocks sticking out from Death's Mountain, and he stained his clothes with mud in the tall grasses. Several times he felt his mind racing ahead of him, trying to break free and leave him right behind. But George was determined and he kept snatching it back. And soon enough George just plain didn't have any energy left to do any more tumbling and so he stopped. When he looked about him he saw that he had landed in a pit of mud, and it came right up to his chest and sucked him down, into the belly of the mountain. He clawed and kicked his way. He thought he might get taken at any moment and he said a thousand prayers. Well, I don't know if any of those angels heard him but he just as well got himself free, catching onto a loose branch hanging from a long-dead tree at the side of the path and he yanked his body up and out. And you know what he saw stretched out before him? Yes, you know, you've heard one too many story, I can see, one or two less than I've heard. Before him he saw Gotsome. All that warm light and those wide streets, those large, new houses, the sounds of singing coming from the public houses.

George was fit to burst, he was.

But before he set one foot in front of the other, and headed down the path into town, he looked back at the mountain, to where he saw Death looming over the side, peering down at him—waiting. And if his breath didn't leave his lungs when he saw him, and if his legs didn't carry him fast as they could down into that town, and to rapping on the doctor's door with both fists, screeching out for help.

And I'll thank you kindly for the sup and be on my way. Old Hella here, he can't be too long outdoors, ain't good for him no more. Nah, he's an inside dog more than I'll ever know. Needs his sleep, just like his master. So I'll thank ya, young 'un, you've got a better heart than most, at least to indulge an old, dying man, and I thank ya for that. What's that ya say? That it wasn't the end? That ya wanna hear whatever happened to George Strangeblood? Well, if that's how ya feel then you know, I could do with . . . why you are a sweet boy. You'll be first in line at the pearly gates, let me tell you that. That's it, set it down right there and I'll take a taste. *Ha!* All this sup's making it so as it's like my birthday. It's the stuff, that's for sure.

George Strangeblood came across the doctor dressed in his nightgown, yawning away and wanting to know what all the fuss was about. And when George told him the doctor wasn't nothing if not a touch reluctant, especially when George insinuated that they were to climb back over Death's Mountain to get to Port Nortle. He shook his head and said, "Nay," and so it was like that George had to make his way himself, the medicine in his hand, wrapped in a brown paper package.

And that was where we met, at the foot of the mountain.

Oh I'm a mite sure that you could've guessed it by now, don't you act dumb, and don't you think about running neither. I'm not in the mood. Do you want to hear the rest of the story or are you all too soused out of your sockets? While you pick your jaw off the bar I'll tell you how it all went down, because goodness knows Hella here needs to get back home.

George Strangeblood saw me standing there with Hella at my heels. He wanted to know if his deal with Death still held up, as if *I* were some sort of shyster. Although I pointed out to him that, really, we hadn't so much as made any sort of deal, I took pity on him and led him the way up that mountain, and then back the other side. Oh, Hella went for his throat a couple of times, but I yanked him back with his collar, and he was quiet. We skittled down the other side and back into Port Nortle, and—don't you just know it?—that storm had not only gone and blown itself out. And George brought that medicine to his sickly daughter and she got all better and everything.

Would you put that bottle down? Someone's gonna get hurt with something so brash. Won't you let an man sozzled on his sup take his leave in peace? Come on Hella, heel, boy. Don't worry, young 'un, you're not seeing things, I am of this world. I am now. For because of my folly in making that deal with George Strangeblood I find myself here, in the mortal realm, to live out a common mortal coil. Good deeds, that's where they get you, at least when we're talking of the hereafter. Now, young 'un, step out of my path and let me by, we'll go our separate ways. Don't you see that the *last* sup never pays? You could've said no, left things as they were, but you had to know more. And you couldn't handle the truth, just like I thought. I'd warn ya, Hella might not look much here, and I might be half broken, but I'll still give you a mighty *whack* between the eyes with my cane. That's it, young 'un, nothing hasty, nothing rash, you let us by right now. We'll go our way here, and you go yours. But promise me one thing, won't ya? You won't let this little episode get in the way of buying an old man a pint of sup.

EAST WING

J IMMY LAY in the spare room of his uncle and aunt's house, with the blankets drawn up to his ears, and hoped the crying in the bathroom would stop. Teddy sat useless to one side. His indifferent eyes and stitched mouth offered no support.

Jimmy listened to his mother's voice, distant and hardly traceable, among the clutched murmurs that floated upstairs; seeming to come from miles under the sea.

The crying in the next room drowned them all out.

What had Jimmy done to deserve this? His mind spun like the spindle of index cards on his mother's desk as he tried to pin down the reason. Perhaps it was the room's smell of cinnamon and glue or the broken windows and peeling paint throughout the house. He recalled this morning he'd tied his right shoe before the left. Maybe that was why he'd had bad luck all day.

The disconnected words of conversation floated under the door and drifted round the room before dropping dead at his feet. Usually, those sounds comforted him—stopped him feeling alone. Tonight, however, it was different. Nothing could save him from the howling figure on the other side of the wall.

The sobs built to a crescendo and his bed vibrated. He tried to clench his teeth, but they continued to chatter—so hard he thought they might crack. The rest of his body shook uncontrollably and the familiar warm sensation crept up between his legs and spread out across the sheets. At first the sensation was pleasant, but soon it became cold and stung. He shivered even more.

He drew a deep breath as the sobs lulled. "Mum!" Jimmy listened for the response, but none came. He called again, louder this time, "Mum!"

The happy voices downstairs dropped the pitch of their discussion. A chair scraped back then footsteps sounded on the stairs. Moments later his mother appeared in the doorway and flicked on the light switch. "What's the matter, poppet?"

"I wet myself."

"Oh dear." She walked over and examined the sheets, her face flushed from wine. "What a shame, and I was just telling Uncle Rick what a good boy you were. Let's get you out of those clothes." His mother pulled the sheets out from under him and Teddy landed on the floor with a *thud*. "Up you come!"

When she lifted him, it pinched his skin, making him wince. She placed him on the wooden floorboards, which felt like ice on the soles of his feet. He glimpsed something at the door and pointed. "What's that?"

"Hmm?" His mother didn't look up as she scrunched the sheets together.

"The bathroom."

She glanced to the door. "Don't be silly, dear, there's nothing there." She slipped the soiled sheets under her arm and took his hand.

His gut clenched as they crossed the floor. What lurked in the bathroom? You didn't disturb crying people. Jimmy knew that. He squeezed his eyes shut as his mother opened the door.

His mother gave him a sharp tug. "Come on, don't muck about!"

He opened his eyes. Nothing. The bathroom was empty. The enormous white tub stood on four silvery legs and the black and white tiles reminded him of the hospital where his grandmother had gone to heaven.

His mother brought him to the sink. She turned on the tap and water spluttered into the basin. "Oh!" She stepped back from the sink in shock. "It's cold!" After a couple of moments, she dangled her hand under the stream and said, "Doesn't seem to be getting warmer, either."

Something rattled through the pipes over their heads and they both looked up.

"Doesn't want to give us hot water, does it?" His mother laughed. "This old house. Ah, well, I'll go and boil the kettle."

Jimmy's heart jolted in his chest. The fear of being left alone here. The monster might come back. "Can I come?"

She shook her head. "Can't have Uncle Rick and Auntie Rosemary seeing you like this, now can we?" She bent down and kissed him on top of the head. "Won't be long, I promise."

He trembled as the cold draught met his urine soaked pyjamas. The hollow room amplified every sound. His ears strained for another sign of the monster, but there was none. He relaxed, hearing footsteps in the corridor.

A euphoric rush ran through him and he looked to the door, expecting his mother. He didn't have much time to register the shock. The wide open mouth, the hollow eyes and the skin stretched to the point of breaking over the bones. He screamed.

When he reopened his eyes, the face was gone and footsteps scuttled up the hall.

"What is it?" His mother stood panting with the steaming kettle in her hands. "What happened?"

Jimmy sobbed and shuddered, fearing the monster might return. He had to warn her. "The monster," he murmured.

She put the kettle down and wrapped him in her arms. "I'm here now." She stroked his hair. "Don't cry."

The familiar rosy smell of her perfume calmed him and he remembered home. The gentle hum of the washing machine, the squeaking garden gate and his mother singing late into the night when she thought he was asleep.

"Let's get you washed and changed."

H IS MOTHER tucked him into bed and left the room.
Jimmy lay there in an unfamiliar set of pyjamas, which she told him once belonged to his cousin Henry. He'd never met Henry. When he'd asked his mother if she had a photo of him she'd said she didn't and not to mention it again because it would make Auntie Rosemary sad. He lay back with Teddy in one hand, and his mind drifted.

A loud *crash* from next door brought him back round. He looked out into the blackness, trying to make sense of the void. He turned over and pulled the cover over his head, not wanting to call out again. It would test his mother's patience and he didn't want to get smacked. Not tonight.

Silence took over. Had he imagined the noise? The face in the bathroom? He hoped so.

Then, *tap* . . . *tap* . . . *tap* . . . the delicate sound came from the pipe directly above his head, like a pendulum ticking back and forth. The door crept ajar a few inches and the light from the hallway lapped at the floor, while the draught blew into the room and bit at his toes.

Should he shut the door? He didn't want to catch a cold. But, was it worth crossing the room? Perhaps the monster lingered behind the door, waiting.

In the end, he decided to shut it. So, with Teddy clutched to his chest, he swung his legs out of bed. As his feet touched the floor, they shook like the leaves on the birch tree at the bottom of his garden. He let go of the blanket, his last connection to the warm safety of his bed, and tiptoed to the door.

He shut the door, listening for the gentle *click* which signalled that it sat snug in its frame. His bed stretched out in the distance and he realised he had to cross the great room again—past the wardrobes and piles of dust covered clothes—to return.

A tickling sensation crawled up his spine as he took one step then another. He jumped the last two steps and fell into the mattress, feeling the old springs creak as they took his weight.

The tapping noise began again. He ignored it.

When he closed his eyes, he saw the face stare back at him— etched on the backs of his eyelids. The figure pressed itself against the ceiling with its head twisted down and its body like a lizard ready to pounce.

3

JIMMY WOKE with a thick head and noticed he'd slept. They'd be going home soon! Out from this nightmarish place! He looked round and realised he couldn't see. It was still dark. His hope faded.

As his eyes adjusted to the darkness, he noticed the door stood wide open. From downstairs the odd tired voice quivered up to his ears, but that wasn't what had awoken him—it had been something in the bathroom. He stepped across the floorboards with Teddy hanging from his hand.

Outside, candlelight flickered at the end of the hallway. He looked to the left. The bathroom door stood open. He went inside. Teddy dropped to the floor and Jimmy screamed until his lungs seared in pain.

His mother lay face down on the floor, her head soaked in a fresh pool of blood.

BROTHERS OF WORD

FRANKENMOORE squeezed his gut in, trying his best to make it past the packed shelves of leather-bound tomes. He inched over to a window, looking down over the castle courtyard.

It was only when he got some moonlight on the subject—*the subject being his stomach*—that he realised he'd been stuck with an arrow.

The funny thing was that there was no pain to accompany this observation, not until his brother—*Tildermoore*—appeared along-side him, and—*unceremoniously*—grabbed hold of the arrow and yanked it free. The pain was searing, unbearable, and Frankenmoore had to remind himself that screaming out would be a Very Bad Idea Indeed.

He consoled himself with biting down hard into his lower lip and making a sort of whimper; the kind that a timid, family mongrel might make.

Often, despite being of noble blood, he believed he had more in common with the mongrel dog than most. Given that he had out-of-control, wiry, blond hair, and a gut which spilled out over his waistband. So little like his brother, Tildermoore, who had done a better job of inheriting the noble 'family' traits: the black hair, the firm, well-chiselled jaw . . . that sort of thing.

Tildermoore let the arrow free of his clenched fist.

It landed at his feet with a twin pair of *clinks*.

Tildermoore dusted his hands as if he'd just completed some laborious task. "That's that, then."

In the moonlight which seeped in through the window, Frankenmoore watched the blood seeping into the material of his tunic. He couldn't help but *feel* that the pain was getting worse by the minute. If it got any more extreme then he wondered if he would faint.

Tildermoore browsed the shelves, his index finger tracing the book spines. He was apparently unfazed by any of this. Then again, why *would* he be?

He hadn't taken an arrow to the gut.

Through flinchingly drawn breaths, Frankenmoore eyed his brother and called him just about every curse under the sun. "It'd better be here. Or else I'm thinking that some defenestration might be in order."

In profile, Tildermoore gave a wry smile. "You should learn to keep your bulk hidden out on the plains, or else a ranger is liable to think you're a rabbit"—he paused for a long moment, closing one eye, peering close to a particular spine before continuing—"or a *boar*."

Frankenmoore said nothing.

He only stared intently at his brother.

Tried not to think about the pain.

Back when they'd been children, their father had put them through various 'knightly' tests; one of which had consisted of 'gauging' their pain threshold. He would perform such tests by, generally, having them experience pain. Their father had administered boiling wax, blades sharp enough to cut through bone, and other such merriment. The tests, he could admit to himself, if not in the presence of his father, had been an abject failure. While his father's stated objective had been that they no longer 'fear' pain, the exact reverse had come true for him . . . he had become acquainted with many different types of pain and so become all the more desperate to avoid them.

Tildermoore, though he might try to hide it behind his dandyish façade, was equally determined to avoid pain of all flavours and types.

Strangely, it seemed that all sorts throughout the kingdom believed that, because their father had been the warrior he'd been, that this talent had somehow managed to pass down to the sons. They didn't seem to be able to comprehend that it could've quite easily skipped their blood . . . where it'd gone exactly, nobody could say for certain . . .

For the most part, Frankenmoore and Tildermoore made it their life goal to avoid finding themselves in perilous situations—the troll-slash-dragon-slash-mage slaying quests were usually politely refused. Once in a while, the odd nonviolent job did come their way: a 'nice little earner', as Tildermoore might've put it. This job—the job on which Frankenmoore had been shot through the stomach with an arrow—had been one of those.

Frankenmoore made a mental note never to pay his brother attention again.

It would've been far simpler if their father had only left them a fortune . . . if they *hadn't* been compelled to take the odd quest here and there to make ends meet.

But it wasn't very well crying about it now.

For one thing, their father being dead, it'd be a waste of tears.

Frankenmoore turned his mind away from the pain, glancing over Tildermoore once again. He narrowed his eyes so that he could better make him out in the gloom. "You found it yet?"

Tildermoore scowled, held a finger up. He continued to scan his current tome. And then, apparently decided, he whipped the book off the shelf. Glanced to the cover. Smiling wickedly, he turned side-on. "I think we're in business."

F RANKENMOORE skirted his brother's heels as they passed through the winding castle corridors. This was something of a contrast to the way they'd entered. Tildermoore, having sized up the locale, and the defensive situation, had declared the best entry point as a partially concealed trapdoor about a mile into the plains —an apparently long-forgotten secret escape route from the castle. And so, *after* Frankenmore had got himself shot in the stomach, the two of them had crawled on their hands and knees through the damp earth.

Frankenmoore had been left with an unsightly tear in the under seam of his trousers.

Not that he'd complained.

He *never* complained . . . or so it seemed.

But that wasn't to say he *wasn't* glad to not be heading back the same way they'd come. The only thing which seemed somewhat dicey was the apparent lack of guile with which they were moving through the castle . . . what would happen when they inevitably ran into some resistance?

Sure enough, he could hear the sound of chatter up ahead. He reached out and grabbed a clump of Tildermoore's tunic in his fist, yanking him back. But when Tildermoore turned to face him, he wore that same wicked smile. "Want to see something fun?"

Although Frankenmoore had his reply sitting on the tip of his tongue—*no*—he couldn't quite manage to get it past his lips. And it was too late.

Instead of taking evasive action, Tildermoore strode nimbly around the corner, the book firmly held in his grasp. Before Frankenmoore could even turn the corner, he heard a guard bark, "Who goes there?!"

His heart jigged in his chest.

His blood ran cold.

But he stood his ground . . . or perhaps *froze* on his ground—more in line with a rabbit than any other animal.

He waited for the whistle of displaced air as a sword was swung. Waited for the warm mist of blood to moisten his cheeks. For the knowledge that *he* would be next to sink in with him. But there was no whistle of displaced air. And no warm mist of blood, either.

In fact, if Frankenmoore had been anywhere else, he might've thought this was merely some polite encounter between, if not good friends, then at least pleasantly minded acquaintances.

With a sigh—the sort of sigh which preludes an inevitable execution—he rounded the corner and found himself at his brother's heels . . . strangely, he saw that the pair of guards were both focussed on the book which Tildermoore held clasped tightly to his chest. Each of the guards bore a spear.

Frankenmoore frowned. He looked to his brother. "What's going on?" he said, feeling a little loath to be the one to break the silence.

The two guards glanced over Frankenmoore very briefly, before turning their gaze back to the book which Tildermoore held.

When Tildermoore spoke to Frankenmoore, his voice was held at a drawl, and although the guards could obviously hear him speaking, it appeared not to matter. "Didn't you read that note I left you?"

Feeling like a fool, Frankenmoore glanced to the guards—their gaze still locked on the book which Tildermoore grasped—and then back to his brother. "No."

"Well, if you *had* done then you would know that this is known as the book that *kills*."

" 'The book that *kills*' ?"

"Uh-huh," Tildermoore said, turning his attention back to the guards . . . even though they still seemed completely enraptured by the book in his hands.

Frankenmoore scoured his mind.

From the reaction of the guards, he could see that whatever Tildermoore said was likely to be close to the truth. How else had he managed to instil such fear in these men?

Tildermoore made a move toward peeling open the book cover.

One of the guards took a step back.

The other—apparently *braver*—merely flinched.

Tildermoore continued to grasp hold of the book cover, as a cut-throat down a side alley might hold a dagger at his thigh. Although Frankenmoore had hardly ever been the blood-thirsty type, he could hardly conceal his desire to see how this book might *possibly* be permitted to kill people.

And that was before he got into the wider issue of just why it'd been stored so carelessly on some apparently anonymous shelf.

"I'll tell you what's going to happen here," Tildermoore said, between gritted teeth.

Neither guard seemed to be much of a mind to contest this.

"You're going to show us the way out of the castle—in fact, you're going to provide us with a private escort."

Neither guard moved from the spot.

They exchanged glances.

Inventorying their options.

Finally, one of the guards, clearly the most loyal—*or the least attached to life*—spoke up.

"Uh, I'm afraid that won't be, er, possible, milord."

Tildermoore had only to give the guard a hard look for him to wither.

"I, uh . . ." the guard replied, and then looked to his colleague, who, as before, apparently had nothing meaningful to contribute.

Tildermoore reached for the book cover again, and this proved enough for the guards to shift free of inaction. The two of them hobbling off the spot, headed around the corner, apparently toward the castle exit.

Tildermoore glanced back at him. "Come on, then. Don't want them escaping, do we?"

3

THE GUARDS LED THEM through the labyrinthine corridors of the castle. With each step, Frankenmoore couldn't help but feel himself growing more and more positive. Throughout these various jobs they'd done, they'd, more often than not, ended up in some sort of dismal circumstance . . . and, to be honest, when Frankenmoore had got himself shot by that arrow, he'd only begun to believe the very worst.

This, though, seemed that it might be an altogether more straightforward affair.

A *welcome* change.

The guards skittled ahead, firing off glances over their shoulders every few seconds or so, apparently constantly wanting to establish the exact location of the book at any given time. Since this *was* a book which could kill people, he could only appreciate their concern.

Finally, they came to what seemed to be a back door; leading out of the castle.

Frankenmoore looked to Tildermoore, who looked right back at him.

Then Tildermoore nodded to the guards.

One of the guards reached for the keys at his belt, then stuck them in through the lock. He twisted, then shoved the door open with a gut-churning *creak*.

Moonlight streamed in through the opening.

Both guards stood back—*way* back—to allow Frankenmoore and Tildermoore through.

It was only when Frankenmoore stood on the grassy bank of the moat outside that he allowed himself to believe that they had *truly* escaped from the castle.

They'd got about a hundred or more paces away from the castle, leaving it behind them, when Frankenmoore finally managed to raise the courage to speak. He even found himself smiling, despite the relatively minor—*apparently*—matter of the arrow hole in his stomach. "So, can I get a look at the book?"

Tildermoore held back a few moments before finally—*reluctantly?*—handing it over.

Frankenmore turned the volume over in his hands, glancing it over, and then, tentatively, he peeled back the cover. Peered at the title page. As he read the title written out there—*A Short History of Gnomish Runes*—he glanced to Tildermoore. "I . . . don't understand."

Tildermoore took the book back. He reached up, tapped his temple with his index finger. "All in the mind, that's the thing."

"What'd you mean?"

"They just needed to *believe* the book would kill them."

He digested this information for several seconds, and then turned his mind back to the wider issue . . . the whole reason *why* they'd shown up here in the first place. "What about the ones who *wanted* the book that kills people?"

Tildermoore shrugged. "As long as we can fob it off to them before they get the chance to test it out it'll be fine. Thing is," he continued, glancing back over his shoulder, "it's all in the threat . . . why'd you kill someone with a book when you've got a spear?"

Frankenmoore supposed, in some weird way, his brother was right. Then again, to be quite honest, his mind was mostly focussed on patching up that hole in his stomach. Already, he couldn't help but anticipate the celebratory, get-well-soon feast.

Whether or not there existed such a thing as a book which killed people seemed beside the point.

THE INFERNAL SERVER

B Y NOW everyone's made up their mind and decided I'm some sort of monster, so I think it's important to put across my side of things.

Let me get this straight: I never wanted to be the one who brought the dead back to wreak havoc on the living.

I was just curious.

My fascination with the dead began about a year ago, just after I'd handed in my final second-year essay on Moore's Law. Stuck in no man's land between the end of term and my summer job at the library, I would go off on YouTube journeys. I'd skim through the standard global conspiracy videos, laugh at extremist rants and argue with strangers in the comments sections.

So it was only natural that I sank into the world of the occult.

One aspect of my YouTube adventures was the documentaries purporting to expose mediums and their methods. Most mediums did turn out to be showmen—frauds cold reading bereaved souls, bringing a bemusing opinion from a deceased nan about their new curtains, or a dodgy picture hanging in the hall.

What perplexed me most about those conversations were the questions people didn't ask. Instead of: 'What's the other side like?' or 'Is there a God?' people would mostly send messages about 'Frank doing well in school' or reiterating that 'Everyone misses them.'

Without wanting to sound insensitive, I couldn't believe the mundane communications between the living and dead worlds, whether they were 'true' connections or not. The whole state of affairs disappointed me. I wanted to know, first, whether the dead could really speak to the living and, second, the answers to some pretty serious questions.

And, just like all my worst ideas, the solution struck me between four and five in the morning, after a night out.

I slumped on the sofa, in the sitting room, smoking weed and playing video games. My housemates had long gone to bed so I was alone. TV light washed over me and I let my eyes lose focus, enjoying the blurry, multi-coloured glow.

In that moment, it seemed a great idea to set up a website where the dead could post messages.

I dropped the video-game controller and trudged upstairs, already writing the page in my mind. It had to be real and it had to be bare bones. An acid test. No trickery, low lights or human interference, like those YouTube frauds.

Straight forward and to the point.

Upstairs, on my laptop, I registered a domain: DeadPeopleStopHere.com, put together a basic page where ghosts could post their message, then signed up to all the major search engines.

All told, it was online in under an hour.

With the sun peeping around the curtains, I crawled into bed and drifted off to sleep.

Over the next few weeks, my YouTube tastes opened up into other areas: reptilian humanoids, the Illuminati and witness accounts from escaped employees of Area 51.

Ghosts floated from the forefront of my mind until one day when I received a message from my web host.

It declared that I'd busted the monthly-usage limit on DeadPeopleStopHere.com and owed a fine.

I had forgotten all about the site.

My mind spun as I typed in the address, wondering what had

possibly caused the upturn in traffic. I was convinced it was hackers or organised trolls.

Worse. Spambots.

I reassured myself that part of my theory was to allow anything in. Using extra software might've meant excluding any *authentic* passing ghoulies. If I were to find just one message amongst the crap it would be a success.

So I kept scanning.

Most of the spam messages gave themselves away—I grew accustomed to picking out: 'penis,' 'Viagra' and 'erection.' Hours later, hands aching and a migraine searing through my temples, I found what I was looking for:

I am dead. Help me.

My blood chilled. I retraced the message, amazed to find something vaguely on topic after hours and hours of scanning spam. Then doubt crept in. It was probably just someone messing around or even just an astute spambot. But I couldn't stop thinking of the consequences, were it true.

I kept searching.

A hundred messages down there was another, dated three days after the first:

Please help me.

If this were a troll, then it was a pretty unimaginative one, a repeated request, no escalation or profanity. That just left the possibility of a spambot. There was only one way to prove whether there was an intelligent being on the other end of these messages and that was with a chat channel. Since the web host had suspended my login, I called them up and paid off the fine with the remnants of my overdraft.

Then I installed a chat application, sat back and waited.

For hours I stared at the cursor, blinking away in the textbox. Nothing. When my stomach rumbled, I set up an audio alert and headed downstairs to make myself a sandwich. There seemed to be some kind of party going on in the sitting room, marijuana smoke blowing under the closed door, but I was so wrapped up in my ghostly computing that I didn't think of joining in.

I got back upstairs to find seven messages waiting:

— *Hello?*

— *Is anyone there?*

— *I want to speak to you.*

— *Please.*

— *Hello?*

— *This is important. I need to speak to you.*

— *HELLO?*

Correct punctuation and perfect grammar. That put paid to any chance of a spambot, or a troll for that matter. What I had on the other end was either a literate—yet deluded—individual or a well-schooled being.

My whole head seemed to buzz as I set my fingers to the keyboard:

— Who are you?

— *I have a message.*

The speakers clicked. I disabled the audio alert and typed out:

— Okay.

— *You who have summoned us. Are you inviting us into your realm?*

— And what if I am?

There was a long pause. I sat staring at the screen for ten minutes, then fifteen. Half an hour passed. Perhaps I had driven the being away. Finally, the response came:

— *I am the keeper. We require a mortal summons to arise. Will you grant us permission to enter the world through the medium you have provided?*

— This website?

— *Yes. We have unfinished business.*

— What business?

— *People forgotten, unfinished quests, loose ends.*

It all sounded suspicious to me. This 'keeper' sounded smug, like some character out of a roleplaying game. I needed some proof.

— Why should I believe you?

A long, long pause and then the lights flickered and went out. My laptop screen turned black. One of my housemates shouted something down the corridor—it was usually my fault when the power tripped.

Something brushed my earlobe, sending a quiver over my skin. I flinched and then heard the words, *"Trust us,"* in a husky whisper.

A few seconds later, the power returned and whatever I had felt in the room with me had left. The light blinked back on. I sat sedated a moment and then I jabbed the power button on my laptop.

My mind swirled.

I began to believe that this was authentic. If so, it would prove my first goal: that there was in fact a land of the dead. But then another revelation sunk in. If this were for real, that I had made contact with the other side, I had to dig in my heels, get some answers.

I brought the page back up and reopened the chat window.

— Okay, I believe you. What is the afterlife like?

— *Pain and suffering.*

Melodrama wasn't exactly what I was looking for, although in hindsight it perhaps wasn't the best approach, asking a inhabitant of 'the beyond' for their opinion of the same, any more than to ask a human their opinion of Earth.

I pressed on, determined not to be blown off course:

— Is there such a thing as God?

— *No.*

I was glad at having got such a straight answer, but the ghoul wasn't finished:

— *At least what you conceive of as God does not exist.*

— Are you God?

— *No.*

This was certainly progress, but I sensed impatience from this 'keeper.' The messages kept coming:

— *Will you permit us entrance to your realm?*

— What will happen if I do?

— *They will leave messages for the living.*

I suppose I should've thought long and hard about the implications of granting that request, but I was riding a wave of revelations, my mind still shaking at the answer to one of life's great questions. And I suppose I also wanted to call the thing's bluff, so I took it further:

— Yes. You may come in.

I expected a word of thanks in the chat window or a purple-black portal to open up in mid-air. I wasn't prepared for nothing.

At midnight, with no more signs of my other-worldly friend, I shut down my laptop and joined my housemates in the sitting room for the nightly spliff and film.

It must've been three or four in the morning when my phone vibrated in my jean pocket. At that point we had the bong out and I had just taken a hit. It was an unknown number but I answered, naively hoping it might be the one girl on my Visual Programming course—the fact she didn't have my number didn't occur to me at the time and, of course, when I answered it wasn't her, but my web host.

If there's one industry in which you never have to speak to anyone, let alone meet face-to-face, it's the web industry.

That was how I knew I was in trouble.

The woman on the line informed me that due to increased traffic they had taken my site offline. Her voice wavered and bobbled—I picked up on her panic. She asked me whether I had insurance to cover the cost, saying the fine might run to five figures. I assured her I did, hung up, switched off then disappeared upstairs, where I spent the night with the duvet over my head, ears pricked for the sound of police sirens.

Since my web host was based in California, and I lived in an ex-council house in the north of England, I doubt they would have rushed in through the door.

But cannabis isn't famed for its ability to ward away paranoia.

It wasn't until the next day that I summoned up the courage to look over the page. And when I did, it just confirmed the phone call from the night before—DeadPeopleStopHere.com had been taken offline—which left the question: what was on there?

In order to reopen the site, and prevent this happening again, I would have to buy my own web server.

Having cleaned out my bank account, I had to get my house-mates involved. Since, like me, they were at the end of term, the idea interested them. Most of them had term-time jobs or parents paying their way, so they comfortably cobbled together two hundred pounds to buy a server.

Only a matter of hours after DeadPeopleStopHere.com was shut down, the Infernal Server went online, with a divert from the old domain.

Now that I'd invited my housemates into the scheme, it was a public affair. Beers in hand, they sat on my bed watching over my shoulder as the messages from the dead ticked down the screen.

This time no one would pull the plug.

Around midnight the whole system went bonkers. Messages poured in. The orange and green lights on the server blinked rapid fire. It seemed that any ghoulies that had got lost on the way to the new site had well and truly found it now.

There was no chance of reading the messages at the speed they came in and my housemates eventually got bored and wandered off to bed.

Although I had let my housemates in on my connection to the spirit world, I hadn't yet revealed my contact, the 'keeper.'

So I waited until that moment to install the chat app on the new site, then typed:

— Are you there?

— *Yes. Why did you break our connection?*

— I got cut off.

— *You must take care with the portal. Do not allow it to come to harm. Keep our haven safe.*

— Why?

— *If the spirits lose their haven, they shall have nowhere to go.*

— Can't they go back to where they came from?

— *No. The ones who have travelled this far may not return.*

— In limbo?

— *Yes. Until they solve their problems in the mortal realm.*

The messages kept the hard drive spinning. New messages rolled in, too quickly to read.

Over the next week, I sat around the sitting room with my housemates, each of us with a laptop cracked open, skimming the messages. All were cries for help. Some mentioned their relatives by name and gave specific requests, while others just screamed out to anyone listening. The messages kept coming, so we bought another server, and another.

Then came to the inevitable day when my housemates approached me, wanting to bring living traffic to the site so we could monetise.

By then, the project had slipped far beyond my grasp, and since I had other people's money involved I felt my hands were tied. I understand that eschewing responsibility isn't attractive to admit, but that's what I did. At first I justified it by telling myself it was a means to break even on the running costs. But, when we did, my housemates wanted more. And I gave it to them.

I promoted the site: selling t-shirts, putting up paid ads and a donation option for those who had resolved their issues with the deceased. Before long, we were generating hundreds of thousands of unique visitors a day and the cash was flowing. I paid off my over-limit fee with my old web host and considered that, if all went well, I wouldn't have to work that summer.

And that was when the service provider came knocking.

A pair of police officers flanked the man at the door. He thrust a legal-looking form in my face and ranted about 'bandwidth hogging' and 'fair-use policies.'

Another, which the policeman carried, detailed a lawsuit for exploitation.

Bemused, I let them in, showed them up to my room where the server whizzed away, messages flowing. I wasn't wholly disappointed they were shutting us down. I had had enough of my spook adventure, and although the money was nice I kind of felt bad about what we were doing—preying off the living's affection for the dead.

The man from the service provider pulled the plug on my server.

And all hell broke loose.

At first it was just a single house alarm on our street, then the sirens on the police car outside blared. Pretty soon the whole neighbourhood shrieked. The police officers' radios went haywire, spitting static and muttering reports and requests.

In the end, they crackled out.

The officers seized me and read me my rights, claiming I'd set off a virus. When I pointed out I'd touched nothing, they slipped on the cuffs and shoved me out the house.

Needless to say, once the techies had looked over the systems, they concluded it wasn't a virus—it was a mega virus.

They held me in the cells.

Every couple of hours some representative of the police, local government or service provider visited, demanding to know what I had done. They taunted me with facts: traffic lights showing green, amber and red at once, train signals failing and navigational systems malfunctioning in planes. One officer even threatened me with extradition to the US.

That one did worry me.

After a few nights of incarceration, when the world had finished panicking, someone asked me nicely for a possible solution and I gave it to them. I argued that the ghosts had fled because their home had been destroyed. That they had to reopen the server and beckon the ghosts back in. Then we could deal with the problem.

So, the servers were returned and I was given a police escort back to the scene of the crime. Of course my housemates had scarpered back to their mummies and daddies at that point, leaving just me in an empty house with a pair of officers for company.

When I got the server back online, I reopened the chat application and typed:

— Please come back.

No response from the keeper. I had no expectation that it would've worked, but it was worth a try. Why would the ghosts return to my cramped server when they had a whole world of cables and airwaves open to them?

We needed something more wide-reaching.

I got in touch with my service provider and asked whether we could send out a worldwide message. They stalled, then someone handed me a phone with the Prime Minister on the other end.

That took me off guard and I struggled to keep my voice steady as I outlined the situation. He made some calls and a plan was set in motion. A message was sent out onto the Web, inviting all the ghouls back to the Infernal Server, where they might live in peace forever after, able to converse with their relatives to their hearts' content.

We sat back and waited.

Messages trickled in, the service provider kept us updated with traffic reports. One thing was certain, the ghosts were migrating, slowly and steadily. We stayed up throughout the night, watching messages dribble over the page.

In the early hours, the service provider called to tell me that the majority of the traffic had returned and they were setting up a network block to prevent the spirits escaping the Infernal Server.

Although I had my doubts of such a system working, I didn't argue.

I was exhausted.

At that point, with the server buzzing, one of the police officers pulled me away from the laptop screen.

A pair of electromagnets in his hands, he knelt down at the server and swiped.

I screamed for him to stop, but he kept going until he had corrupted the disc.

Ten minutes later, the police packed up and left.

I refreshed InfernalServer.com:

404 Error

I can't say I wasn't relieved it was all over, but I felt for those souls: living and dead, who had lost their connection. The irony of the whole episode was that I had been left with more questions than when I started.

Where had the spirits gone?

Had they simply disintegrated into thin air?

What about the keeper?

I had no answers.

The world rebuilt itself over the summer and returned, more or less, to normal.

Politicians explained away the various blips, blaming anarchist hackers—me and my site for letting them in. But, after a lengthy investigation, they left me alone.

I got the impression the Prime Minster had had a word in someone's ear.

And so, I packed up and left the student house, back to my library summer job, glad to be surrounded by paper and glue, rather than electronics and ghouls.

But, even there, I couldn't escape.

I recall one evening, shelving books at around ten o'clock at night. Something brushed my neck and whispered in my ear, "*We need you. Forever.*"

The unmistakable voice of the keeper.

I clung to the book and looked around.

But there was nothing to see.

I have no idea of the range and influence of the keeper, all I know is that whenever a rogue ghost crops up on the Web it's explained away to the public as a virus, spam or bad-coding practice.

But I'm the one they call.

A BRUSH WITH DESTINY, A DEAL WITH FATE

THERE WERE FEW THINGS bleaker than the fairground, or so Randall Williams thought as he took his seat opposite the psychic. The tent was propped up by several flimsy-looking rafters, about as thick as toothpicks. The material of the tent itself was mauve with little silver, reflective stars stitched into it, and there was a mildew smell clinging to the place. A single light bulb dangled from the roof on an unlikely cocktail of variously coloured wires, all twined one around the other.

Randall eyed his watch, knowing that he had another good half an hour to burn. His wife and children were great fans of fairgrounds and so he had taken the noble decision to leave them to it, not wanting to stomp all over their one-day-a-year of fairground fun with his dour mood. And so he found himself right here, in the psychic's tent, having been ushered in by a dwarf dressed-up as an Edwardian gentleman.

That was the last time he would trust a dwarf.

The psychic herself had those deeply embedded wrinkles that you would just believe were sketched on there by design, and her skin was so leathery that it took Randall a colossal leap of belief to think that she hadn't contrived to dry it out like that. In a way he would've liked to have touched it to see if it really had the same texture as a leather jacket.

He had that too-sweet taste of candyfloss stuck in his teeth and smothering his tongue, his children had also managed to get him to buy them each a toffee apple, and after they'd taken a couple of licks each before deciding they couldn't finish it, and what with Randall's wife Karen watching her figure and Randall himself hating to see things go to waste, he'd eaten the damn thing himself. His stomach rumbled with the memory.

Outside he could hear the cross-chatter prattle of the folk who ran this fairground, calling out for people to try their game, to try their luck or try . . . well, they mostly just wanted people to try.

And to pay for the privilege.

The psychic sat in her chair, eyelids either closed or narrowly open. Randall wasn't sure which. She had her hands reaching forward touching the crystal ball between the two of them, her fingers spread out to clutch it as if she were burying her hands in a favourite cat's stomach.

He was fairly certain she was a *cat* person.

Randall looked about him, already feeling the creepers of boredom beginning to take root. Not much else in the tent, to be honest. There was the half-burned-out joss stick which sat on the table behind her, which, after Randall had coughed a good three or four dozen times, she'd offered to extinguish for the duration of their meeting. Then there was the skull beside the joss sticks, the colour of jaundice, which sent shudders through Randall's muscles and made him wince just to look at it. And finally, or the final item that Randall *dared* take in, was the jar which seemed to contain some unspecified animal embryo in whatever green goo it was they used to preserve these things.

Formaldehyde was it?

Did it really matter?

The psychic, Psychic . . . Phony, whatever name he wished to tag her with, was now lightly humming, her fingers still stretched out over that crystal ball, which to Randall still seemed very much like an ornament one of his grandmothers had had on her mantel-piece, the same one he'd broken playing football in the house with his brother. He guessed the only reason he remembered that orna-ment, and breaking it, was because of the bruises he'd had on his backside for the rest of the summer. Old people didn't tend to have much of a sense of humour about crap like that and breaking it, and

Randall had made a mental note to himself, there and then, not to metamorphose into that sort of third-age being.

But that was all very well in theory.

Randall rocked back in his chair and took to looking at the ceiling again. His mouth was watering and he knew that he desperately needed an injection of some protein or other. That burger van with the brown-sauce grease stain down the front of it that sat just on the fringe of the fairground, neither part of it, nor not part of it, now seemed mightily appetising to him. The man who'd run it had been especially horrible. What with that seven-day stubble and the sweat stains pooling around the radiuses of his armpits. And yet he could almost taste that greasy, sloppy, meaty hamburger already. He could smell that meaty stench, hear the *sizzle* of the onions and the slight *sigh* of the melting cheese. Feel the sweaty warmth in his hands.

Randall eyed the psychic. Maybe he could just sneak out—blow her off. This might be his last chance. As he flexed his calves, got his middle-aged body ready for lift off, the psychic, all of a sudden, fluttered her eyelids open and looked at him with a maniacal smile.

There are few scarier times than knowing that you're simply locked down by someone smiling at you maniacally, that there's just no place to escape to. And it's fair to say that Randall felt just as you might expect. He scoped out the exits, those fear sweats already coming on, and a thousand stray thoughts all rushed through his brain, including, but not limited to: knocking the old lady over then ploughing out through the tent, grabbing a fistful of joss sticks and torching the damn place, simply just getting up, making his excuses, and leaving. However, Randall, being somewhat passive, even laid-back to the untrained eye, he just sat there, planted in that seat, pinned by that maniacal smile.

He took in her features. She had mascara smudged on about her eyes, the same mauve as the tent itself. And her perfume for some reason now became almost overpowering. A scent of lilacs clawed at his nostrils, made his head swirl. The sounds outside still sounded but it was like someone had stuffed damp cotton balls in his ears, and the only clear sound he could hear was what the psychic had to say.

"*You*," she said, stretching the word out in that way old crones can do. "You aren't a believer in Fate. Destiny. Are you?"

Randall had to admit that she'd got him there. But he wasn't about to let on lest she turf him out. And whatever else happened, he was determined to get his money's worth from all of that two-pound-fifty the dwarf had somehow expunged from him.

That was another thing that bothered him about the fairground —the chucking money away on tat and idiocy.

She cocked her head to one side and looked at him with squinty eyes. He was sure he could hear her spittle bubbling on her tongue and crackling in her throat.

"Um," Randall said, "I, well"—*ah, the hell with it*—"no, I'm not, actually."

Her eyes flared and she sat back in her seat with pouty lips, eyeing him through the spectacles he'd only just realised she was wearing. They had those beads connected to either of the arms, and the chain draped around her neck, he supposed, so she didn't lose them. A wry smile slithered across her lips. "You can go, if you want. If you're not interested."

Randall pondered this, thought about what she was getting at exactly. He thought about the time he still had to burn, the other possible distractions. He was sure there might be other dwarves out there, ready to lead him astray, perhaps into something worse.

Or into something even *more* expensive.

He tried to prop his elbow onto the back of his chair, but failed, realising that the back of the chair was actually several inches above his head—one of those high-backed chairs, big and bulky oak. It must've weighed a ton. Or maybe they shipped it from town to town using magic. He managed a shake of the head and a slight tweak of the lips that looked, and was, an unconvincing smile.

"You're sure you want to stay?" she said.

"Yes," Randall replied.

"All right then, we shall begin."

2

A KNOT FORMED in Randall's throat and he felt his stomach rumble. He would go for a hamburger after this nonsense, that sounded like a good plan. By then it would *surely* be time for them to go home.

And that would be the end of it for another year.

No more fairgrounds for a while.

The psychic tapped the surface of the table with her long fingernails—also mauve—and made a horrid scratching type noise against the silk, turquoise tablecloth as she did so. It took Randall another few seconds before he realised he was supposed to put his own hand on the table, which he did so now.

He stared at his hand on the table, like an arctic explorer making peace with an appendage soon to be lost to frostbite. He looked to the psychic for direction.

She uncurled her hand, those knobbly fingers that reminded him of twigs lying on a forest floor. "Don't be shy, dear," she said.

He wasn't, reaching over and lying his palm flat against her own. She clasped his fingers so their hands formed a kind of S shape. Her touch was strangely warm, and comforting, in a strange way. Randall decided that this psychic reminded him of his grandmother . . . on the other side, the one which hadn't beaten his backside black and blue.

The psychic shut her eyes again and made that light humming sound again. After a second or so she crooked open an eyelid and said, in a slightly frosty tone, "Close your eyes, please."

"Oh," Randall said, then did as she asked.

It was strange, the first few seconds nothing at all remarkable happened. He thought he could feel a light vibration passing through his chest, but took that as hunger. He felt at peace with himself, that same warmth passing through him. And the lilac perfume let off him just a little, stopped ticking his nostril hair. Then he had the sensation of floating, of moving upward. He tried to open his eyes but couldn't. He was sure, if he could just reach out, his fingertips would be brushing the roof of the tent.

"Dear? Dear?"

The words drifted back to him as if he was lying in the middle of a tranquil ocean, lying flat on an inflatable raft. Randall continued to float there for a little while, till he had the sharp sensation of the psychic digging her fingernails into his palm.

"Ouch!" Randall said, coming out of the trance, or whatever it was she'd done to him. Then he realised that, if he really couldn't before, he could now open his eyes. And when he did he wasn't all that pleased with the results. He saw that the psychic was frowning at him. Before he had even let her get a word in edge-ways, he found himself saying, "What? What is it? What's the matter?"

She pressed her lips together, forcing a half-smile, but it was clear that it was grim news indeed. She gave the crystal ball a cursory glance then clasped her hands together, intertwining those twig-like fingers. That lilac perfume was back with a vengeance and Randall had the sudden urge to sneeze. But he held it in.

"Death," she said.

A tingle ran up Randall's spine. "Come again?"

"Death."

The sounds of the fairground around him rushed back. Those barking hawkers, the children screaming out with pleasure on the gigantic inflatable slide, and, he was almost sure of this, he could hear the heavy breathing of the dwarf on the other side of the tent flap.

He took in the psychic before him then said, "Care to elaborate?"

She just gave him a vacant glance. And then he saw the opened palm lying on the table before her.

He was sure this was a trick, a ruse to get the customer to part with the money. And yet . . . something about this whole situation, all that *floating* business, had put him on his guard. Now he *had* to know what it was she was up to. He sifted through his change in his pocket, slipped out a shiny new pound, one which he'd hoped might contribute toward that long-promised hamburger, and he crossed the wench's palm with silver.

Or whatever metal it was they made pound coins with.

She gave him a slight smile. Her fingers wrapped around the pound coin like a boa constrictor draping itself around a vole—just for a cuddle. Seconds later the coin was gone. Dropped into some purse she kept at her belt, out of sight by the fold of her floral blouse. She settled her hands before her on the table and looked him in the eye. "You are going to die," she said, quite plainly, and without the emotional weight this statement might demand.

"Right," Randall said, "I think that's what you said before. Care to get a little more specific?"

She threw her hands up and spread her fingers—it made Randall think of a flock of baby pigeons taking flight for the first time. "Oh, *the shadows* they are so vague and twisted and *oblique*—the thinning of the veil of the domain of the *living*, and that of the *dead*, it is so highly guarded by Him, the most wicked of the wanderers, the most—"

Randall fished into his pocket and plonked a scattering of pound coins on the table between them.

The psychic wrapped the melodrama up pretty swiftly, dropping the high tones and lowering her voice to that of plain speak. "Thirteen days," she said. "That is all. Nothing more, nothing less. Thirteen days."

Randall furrowed his brow as she swept the pound coins off the table, raking them into her palm before depositing them into that purse she kept at her belt, along with the rest of his purloined coinage.

"Sorry?" he said. "Thirteen days? Why thirteen days? How can you be so sure? How will I die?"

She held up her palm and sealed her eyes tight as if taking some sort of communiqué from whatever spirit was feeding her this information. She parted her lips and opened her eyes wide, almost glaring at him. Her lilac perfume was ripe, pungent even now. "It shall be a watery death. A *watery* death."

This was probably enough. That burger was all but impossible to resist now, and so Randall arched an eyebrow and rose from his seat. "Guess I'd better stay clear of swimming pools, then." He cast her a parting glance at the flap of the tent. "Thanks for . . . whatever, this was."

She remained there, sitting in her seat, her eyes glowering out at him like a pair of hot coals. He was sure that the skull on the table behind her was staring at him too.

Mind you, those joss sticks weren't without their menace either.

"Stay away from the water," she said.

He gave her a light smile. "Will do."

3

OUTSIDE, the dwarf, still in his Edwardian costume, awaited Randall with a wry smile on his lips.

Randall smelled smoke and realised that the dwarf had a cigarette trapped between his stubby fingers. Randall sniffed a couple of times, never able to stomach normal smoke, let alone the special chemical variety they packed into cigarettes.

The dwarf's smile widened. "Get your money's worth with Mistress Margaret, then, or what?"

Although the dwarf attempted to speak in a period accent, it frequently descended into his—obviously native—cockney one. And it was a little high pitched too, like dwarfs' voices tend to be.

Randall side-stepped the slightly sordid insinuation of the question and said, "It passed the time."

"Yes," the dwarf said, his grin widening. "It certainly did."

"Should you, I mean, are you meant to smoke those?"

"What?" the dwarf said, holding up his cigarette, wafting it almost in Randall's face—some achievement given his diminutive forearms. "This?" He snorted then blew out a cloud of bluish smoke, exposing yellowing teeth. "I'm an adult, course I can do what I want."

Randall gave the dwarf a polite smile and then wandered off, back among the fairground. When he looked back over his shoulder he noted that the dwarf was still staring at him, with that same maniacal grin that the psychic—Mistress Margaret—had treated him to.

Randall found his wife Karen and his children, Jasper and Pipple, short for Penelope. He had had no role in naming them, of course, and his wife obviously had high aspirations for them, which wasn't to say that he didn't share those aspirations, but he didn't have all that much interest in moving in social circles with people called either Penelope or Jasper.

Funny what scars a working-class upbringing could leave on you.

Or maybe it was just good taste.

Karen was wearing her white cotton dress that she always dragged out for these yearly trips to the fairground. It made her look youthful—like a young girl again. Her cheeks were slightly flushed and her black hair had gone all frizzy, apparently from an excess of fun.

When he leaned in to give her a peck on the lips, he tasted and smelled her sweat. Again, it made him think that she was being a girl again. And he was glad for her, even a little miffed that he somehow couldn't share her enjoyment of the fairground . . . or the enjoyment of his children.

"What've you been up to?" Karen said.

"Oh, this and that," Randall said with a shrug. "Just pottering about really."

She smiled easily at him. "Sorry about dragging you here, I know you don't like it. Tomorrow we'll do something you want to do."

Tomorrow was Sunday, and the first of the thirteen days the psychic had told him about. That was unless she had been counting today too, otherwise, seeing as it was now about seven thirty in the evening, he would have thirteen-and-four-fifths days to go.

That must be it because otherwise he would've only had twelve and one fifth days to go.

Then again, he didn't suppose that one became a psychic with a solid grasp of mental arithmetic. Or maybe the spirits, or whatever, had done the arithmetic for her.

Or perhaps, just perhaps, it was all just piffle and he should just stop thinking about it.

4

O N THE CAR RIDE HOME, Randall wound down his window despite Karen's protests, and Pipple claiming she was cold.

In any case, about five minutes away from the wretched fairground, they were all asleep.

Randall savoured the fresh night air on his face, breathing it in, feeling himself exhaling all those warm, unpleasant stenches of the fairground—getting well-shot of that buttered popcorn odour, that sticky candyfloss which would take him about ten minutes of tooth brushing with floor polish to get out of his mouth, and, of course, that incessant lilac perfume that psychic had been wearing.

Karen had commented briefly on it, and it had worried Randall momentarily, that she might take it another way—think that he'd somehow scheduled some sort of liaison with another woman.

An *older* woman.

But Karen had only remarked that it had reminded her of an old aunt, the same perfume she'd once used, and said nothing more.

The air made slight chopping sounds as it poured in over the window and into the car. He kept the wheel steady in his hands, guiding the car around the grassy-banked country lanes. The moon shining above, like a jaundiced eye, his only company. What was it with him and jaundice today?

No wonder that psychic had pronounced death upon him.

She could probably smell it all over him.

. . . And there he was thinking about it all over again.

Why couldn't he just put it out of his mind?

5

THAT NIGHT, he lay in bed with Karen. The kids were in bed, and soon after they'd each given them a kiss goodnight, he and Karen had shared a nightcap. She'd soon slipped out of that pristine white dress, fairground smells still sticking to it, and draped it over a chair in the corner of the room. Then she'd tucked herself into bed and waited for him.

Well, she hadn't had to wait too long.

Or too long after *that* either.

As they lay there, she with her head propped up on his chest, breathing deeply, clearly on the cusp of sleep, Randall found himself feeling wide-awake, staring at the ceiling. On impulse, he craned his neck back down and caught the clock changing from 11.59 to midnight. Its neon-red LEDs declaring that, as of right now, he had thirteen days to live.

If fairground psychics were to be believed.

Which was a *big* if.

6

I T WAS FUNNY, that psychic bothered Randall all through the next day.

True to her promise, Karen let him have his own way, and got them going on a walk alongside a disused canal nearby. Despite the lush overgrown grass which stuck up in tufts, the merry twitters of the wrens flying overhead and the broad shining sun, he just couldn't bring himself to let go of what it was the psychic had said to him.

At the end of the walk, with the children running free, headed for the car they saw parked up ahead, Karen turned into him and asked, "What's the matter with you today?"

Randall took in a lungful of the fresh air, feeling that nice and cold sensation in his mouth, then he blew it out again—just like that dwarf had exhaled that cigarette of his. It was nice out here, it really had cleansed his whole . . . well, he wouldn't say spirit, because he just plain didn't believe in that sort of thing, but he could say that those unpleasant memories of the smells, sounds and tastes of the fairground were now a long way away—relegated to far-forward thinking, knowing he wouldn't need to suffer them again till next year.

As another wren twittered merrily overhead, bobbing gently as it barrelled through the air, he turned to Karen, smiling to himself. "Oh, nothing. I'm fine."

She gave him a stiff look, glanced ahead to the children, obviously a little concerned that they might overshoot the car park and run out onto the main road. At that moment they were occupied looking down into a grassy ditch, looking at some bugs or something.

"You've hardly said anything all afternoon," Karen said.

"What does that mean?" Randall replied.

"Well, on these walks you're usually chattering on about something or other."

This remark vexed Randall a touch. Just the tone of it more than anything else, although he did have to admit that the bloody psychic's words had some effect on his mind. "Sorry to disappoint," he said, gazing at the beaten track leading to the car park.

Karen rolled her eyes. "Oh, don't be all precious about it." She reached out and laid her hand on his back, between his shoulder blades. "I'm just wondering if there's something on your mind, that's all."

They carried on for a few more silent steps. Randall thought about raising the topic of the psychic with Karen, but just couldn't bring himself to do it. To begin with it would be terribly awkward to admit that he'd allowed that damn dwarf to trick him into her tent in the first place, and after all he'd chided her about her own peculiarities, her claims that there were certain plants in the garden that carried certain 'energies' or particular colours that summoned up 'feelings.' It would have been akin to waving the white flag on this sceptical war he was waging.

Admitting that he, too, had a tendency toward the kooky.

No, better to just keep schtum, like his father had always taught him by example—that was how he'd kept himself out of trouble with his mother at least.

"Randy?" she said. "You're doing it again."

"Doing what again?"

"You know, you've gone all quiet."

Randall stared out ahead of him. They were approaching the kids now, still staring down into that ditch. He listened to the slight *scuff* of the soles of his shoes as he passed onto tarmac, the beginnings of the car park, and he got that slightly queasy feeling in his stomach at the prospect that he would soon be a passenger in the car—he always did think Karen drove too fast, too recklessly, not that he would ever tell her so.

He thought he could already taste the first strains of vomit at the back of his throat, feel his limbs go all floaty at the prospect.

Karen turned away from him and clapped her hands at the kids. "Come on," she said. "Time to go. It's almost tea time."

However, both Pipple and Jasper remained transfixed by the ditch, both of them doubled over, hands pressed to their kneecaps. Only another smart *clap!* from Karen caused Pipple to look up at them. "Come look," she said.

Karen glanced back at Randall, gave him a slight grin. Then she grasped hold of his hand. Her hand felt cold, and a little moist. Almost like it was a stranger's hand. But he allowed her to tug him along, over to the lip of the ditch where Pipple and Jasper waited.

As Karen drew up to the edge, and her eyes ran along whatever it was in there, she released Randall's hand and it went up to her lips. She gasped at the sight.

Randall felt his stomach dip, the sensation that only suggests you're about to see something horrible, something that's going to shake your bones.

He drew up alongside Karen and looked down.

There, at the bottom of the ditch, was a wren, lying on its back. Its eyes were clasped tight and it was beating its wings spasmodically. Its chest was vibrating as its tiny heart struggled to keep up with its panic.

Randall felt his own chest tighten, his own heart rate double. He felt all his muscles stiffen and his brain go all fuzzy. Suddenly the wind grew cold—impossibly cold—and his hearing was filled with a thousand ringing bells. He felt himself grow numb, slowly from his extremities—his fingers and toes—before it seeped over him, like lapping water, and the rest of his body followed.

He heard Karen's voice, watched her putting her arms around

each child's shoulders before guiding them away to the car. She shot Randall a glance, again with that slight, knowing smile. Then she shepherded them away.

All of a sudden, the wren ceased moving.

Its wings stilled and its beak opened slightly as it gave its last breath.

Randall was sick in one, thick warm flow. It tasted like acid in his mouth. As he was sick, he kept himself facing away from Karen and the kids, and none of them looked back. When he was done, with the base of his stomach feeling like a pit of lava, he wiped his mouth with the back of his hand and followed after them.

7

WORK, thankfully, didn't give Randall such brutal hints about his mortality. In fact, he supposed that the glare of his computer screen acted as a sort of brain-wiping ray. He just stared at the endless lines of code, clicking here and there, typing in flurries and droughts, pausing to see whether what he'd written made any sense.

And in those delightful moments the psychic was forgotten.

Or so he thought.

When he went off on his coffee break, propped himself up against the heavily-stained kitchenette counter, his steaming mug in his hand, he found his mind sweeping back to the psychic, back to what she'd told him. That it would be a *watery* death. And he had told her he wouldn't go swimming. He'd sounded so blasé about the whole thing, and now *look* at him, a nervous wreck.

He finished his black coffee, taking down every last drop of liquid, forcing himself to even swallow the grains which always seemed to sneak their way through the filter, then he deposited his cup in the sink with a dull *chink* of porcelain on stainless steel.

And then he was back at his computer, forgetting again.

8

THROUGHOUT the week Randall maintained this morbid fascination.

Unconsciously, every morning on seeing the date written out on the LCD display of the digital clock in his bedroom, counting off another day.

In the evenings, when he got home from work, he was totally distracted. Dinner tasted like ash in his mouth and he had to force himself to finish it all. He gave up on drinking his evening glass of red wine in front of the TV, Karen propped up against his shoulder, because it tasted like vinegar in his mouth.

Even when he kissed either of his children, or pressed himself up against his wife every night, he felt that heat becoming so scorching and uncomfortable that he had to extricate himself at the earliest opportunity.

Sleep, of course, also became a major issue, which was to say that he couldn't sleep at all. More than once that week, Karen kicked him out of bed, sent him to sleep in the guest bedroom for persistent rolling around, tangling the blankets all over the place. Only later did he get the trick of lying still, staring up at the ceiling, and waiting for the first light of dawn to come.

He stayed silent about the whole matter till, on the day before the psychic had told him he would die a watery death, he decided that enough was enough, that he had to swallow his pride and confront his wife—confide in her.

As far as nights went, it was a slightly complicated one, given that Jasper was performing in a school play that evening—something one of the teacher's had knocked together. It was big on moral and deficient on plot, Randall thought.

But what did he, a humble computer programmer, know . . .

They got back through the door around ten in the evening. Both kids were shattered. But especially Pipple, who had had to suffer through her brother's play, had needed to sit still, for about ninety minutes. They forwent the bath that evening, and Randall and Karen put them both to bed.

Both kids went out just as quickly as the smart *click* of the light switch in each of their respective bedrooms.

Karen gave a gigantic yawn, and Randall smelled the fresh, apple-scented perfume she wore. Tonight she'd worn a sea-blue dress over jeans, a pair of sandals down below. Randall had thought she'd looked the most sophisticated, and the sexiest, of all the other mummies there. But that brief distraction left him now, knowing that he had to be honest with her.

After all, if the psychic was right, it might be the last chance he ever got to be.

Just as Karen turned on her heel, headed for the bathroom, to brush her teeth and change into her pyjamas, Randall found himself reaching out and curling his fingers around her arm. Maybe it was the lack of sleep and the pent-up tension, all the waiting to finally confront her, but he squeezed quite hard. Hard enough that she winced and looked at him with a slight frostiness in her eyes. He was so taken off guard by her response that he took his hand off her immediately, feeling his fingertips slip away from her butter-smooth skin.

"What?" she said, dropping her fright now, and allowing concern to creep into her voice. "What's the matter?"

And so he told her, right from the start, the whole fairground deal—all about the dwarf and the psychic, even the part where the psychic had managed to swindle him out of a good deal of his shrapnel.

As Randall related this to Karen, she stared at him intently, lips pressed tightly together, only her motion of breathing breaking her image of total and complete concentration.

When he finished, she gazed at him with wide eyes, then she squeezed them shut and pressed her fingers to the backs of her closed eyelids. Her shoulders shook and Randall was absolutely certain that she was silently weeping. And then she tilted her face up to him, and he saw the grin there, the light shining in her eyes, defying the dark bags below.

She let loose a giggle and then more and more, waves and waves of giggles.

For a second Randall was absolutely furious. Although a cliché, he actually saw that flash of red cloud his vision, the tension all crunched up and bursting to get out somehow. But he kept it inside himself. And then, as his brain took over once more, reminded him of the ridiculousness of the situation, he found himself laughing along.

It seemed like hours stretched by with the two of them there, in that corridor lit only by a dim, tangerine-coloured nightlight, with the light snores of their children drifting around their half-closed doors. They snickered to themselves at the sheer idiocy of the whole thing.

And then, still stifling their laughter, they went to bed, so as not to wake the children.

That night, Randall slept soundly till his alarm clock woke him at his regular six thirty the following morning. And he was a refreshed man, filled back up with vitality, positivity, and any other -*ivities*, you'd care to mention.

If only he'd looked ahead, checked the calendar, and seen that, the following day, Pipple's first swimming gala was written there in Karen's curly handwriting.

9

THERE WAS A BRIEF, but frosty, discussion between Randall and Karen the following evening.

Randall tried his best to put his view forward, to tell Karen that, although what the psychic had said to him was obviously ridiculous, and they'd now had a great laugh about it, he just couldn't face tempting fate. They arrived at a compromise, which involved much eye-rolling on Karen's part. At the back of his mind, Randall admitted that he couldn't really blame her.

He was starting to sound like a mad man.

And so they all piled into the car, with Pipple already wearing her swimming costume below her clothes, and talking a mile a minute about what was planned for the gala. He noted Jasper looking out the window, chin propped up in his hand, and sighing loudly.

Randall couldn't help a wry smile, both at the fact that his son was getting older, already showing those teenage signs, and also at the fact that he might well get to see him as a teenager after all.

As they'd agreed, Randall dropped them off at the school gates, waving them off. There was a lot of frowning from Pipple, lots of her asking Mummy why Daddy wasn't coming to see her. He overheard Karen say something along the lines of Daddy having some very important work to do. Jasper complained that Daddy was getting to duck out of what was going to be an *extremely* boring engagement. And Karen fed him something along the lines of Pipple having gone to see Jasper's play the night before. Just as Randall pulled away from the curb, he caught a stern glance from Karen. And he thought he saw another eye roll too. But he didn't care.

It was better to be safe than sorry.

He drove around the neighbourhood, clicking on the radio to some sports talk show. He wasn't sure which sport they were discussing and, to be honest, it really didn't matter. He just wanted to hear something, and mindless sports prattle was just a notch more tolerable than white noise—and just as vapid.

He took care to steer clear of any bridges, especially ones with gushing streams down below, and looked out for any sign of rain clouds gathering overhead.

But he was in luck.

It was a clear night.

Nevertheless, he paid attention to the road at all times, some odd mechanism within him hinting that he should doubt the psychic's confident prediction that it would be water that would do him in.

If he was going to be this wary of her words, he wasn't going to take any chances.

About two hours later he drove back along the old familiar road to the school. He kept his speed to around twenty-five miles an hour, slowed right down for each individual speed bump, and kept an ear out, over the incessant babble of the radio, for any lorries that might arrive unexpectedly, driving at top speed, from one of the side roads.

As he turned the corner onto the road which ran alongside the school, he was immediately struck by the flashing red-and-blue lights up ahead. At first he crumpled his forehead, unable to quite understand what it was he was seeing.

And then he made sense of those letters stencilled clearly in fluorescent lettering on the side of the flashing van.

AMBULANCE

10

R ANDALL'S HEART throbbed in his throat. He felt his stomach drop right through the car seat. He gripped the wheel so tight that the tips of his fingers turned white. Again he had that ashen taste in his mouth and, strangely, that sweet stench of candyfloss through the nostrils. As he drew closer, coasting now, merely guiding the car forward, unable to summon the strength of mind to press his foot to the accelerator, he heard the animated voices, the sound of everyone talking at once. It reminded him of people coming out of a concert, all chatting animatedly. However, in this case, as he parked up the car and flung off his seatbelt, listening to the *whizz* and *snick* of the mechanism as he did so, he saw that they were parents, putting their arms around the shoulders of their children, who had their faces in their hands, guiding them away from the school.

Randall stumbled as he jumped from the car. He landed with a *smack* on the pavement, his forehead smashing into asphalt.

Dull pain ripped through his skull.

He pulled himself up into a crouching position.

His head felt like a well-stuffed pillowcase.

Someone appeared before him, a woman—a mother—asking him whether he was all right, and then saying something else that he couldn't understand. She was frantic, her words impossible to understand. Randall dodged around her, moved his attention to the parents and children streaming out through the school doors.

He felt like a salmon going upstream, pushing past all these people. He looked for familiar faces in the crowd, spotted several, other children, friends of his children's and their parents—but all just acquaintances.

Where were Pipple and Jasper and Karen?

When he got inside the building, the crowds thinned slightly. There was a scent of floor polish in the air, and he guessed the cleaners had just finished up for the night. He looked along the corridor, to the double glass doors which led to the pool beyond. His head still thumping, his mind racing with a thousand different possibilities, he ran on, feeling his feet slip several times below him on the freshly polished floor.

Just as he reached the doors, laid his hand up against the impossibly cold metal plate to push one of them open, he saw Pipple and Jasper on the other side, being led by a mother that he vaguely recognised—perhaps one of her kids had come over once, or he'd gone to pick either Jasper or Pipple up from her house.

Her face was grave, her complexion pasty, and a light layer of sweat shone under the fluorescent light.

Randall propped the door open for her to pass through, too exasperated to even form words. The lady could only shake her head. And then he saw the tear tracks running down either cheek. She held both Jasper and Pipple to her hips, a hand on the side of either's face. Pipple was still dressed in her pink swimming costume with the frilly hem.

Randall felt torn. He looked to his children, but both of them had their eyes closed, apparently lost in their own thoughts, with the lady holding them at her hips. He hesitated, and then, with the lady sobbing something to him, words he couldn't understand, he ploughed on into the swimming pool.

There were several puddles lying about and Randall splashed through them, dimly aware that he was soaking the legs of his jeans. He stood on the spot and pivoted, taking the place in.

And then, all of a sudden, he saw the paramedics, two of them, both dressed in high-vis green jackets, kneeing over a person laid flat at the poolside.

Randall's heart skipped several beats and his head throbbed

from the pain, from where he'd hit it against the pavement. As he walked, he listened to his wet footprints echo around the pool area.

One of the paramedics glanced back over her shoulder, looked to Randall and said, "Wait outside, please, sir."

But then Randall saw beyond her, he saw the face of his wife.

Karen's face.

She was lying there, prostrate, lifeless. Her head draped to one side. She had a bandage wrapped around her head. Blood spotted the pristine white. This time Randall did manage to get out words. "I . . . I'm her husband."

Both paramedics turned to look at him, their thin, bloodless lips telling him everything he needed to know.

His throat felt dry. ". . . How?"

They exchanged glances, then the female paramedic spoke. She had blond hair and hazel eyes. She wore her hair up in a bun at the back of her head. Although she was thin and she had hardly any wrinkles, there was a weariness about her. Something that told Randall that she was probably older than he thought. She regarded him from where she crouched. "One of the kids," she said. "She saw one of them fall into the pool. She jumped after them—tried to save them from drowning."

Randall felt his whole body cool, his heart was like a slab of concrete and his arms were like lead weights, dragging down at his sides.

All of a sudden, he felt heat flood into his cheeks, take over his brain, send him dizzy. It was like he'd knocked back half a bottle of whisky.

He wanted to vomit, to get it all out in one acidic stream, but the more he thought about it, the more he realised that he no longer had the strength to do so.

And then he just turned and walked away.

11

THE LADY, the one who had taken Pipple and Jasper away, it turned out, was called Angela. She was the mother of one of Jasper's friends and she agreed without resistance to take them both home with her that night.

Randall bent down and gave them each a soft, tender kiss on their foreheads. He savoured their soft skin and the light shudder that passed through them as he kissed them both.

Then he got in the car and drove.

As he blazed along the country lanes, he thought about things from Angela's perspective. He thought about it almost in *chiding* retrospect—wondering just what she must've been thinking to let a recently bereaved husband go off alone.

Then again, he guessed, having watched Karen die, having watched the life blood seep out of her, Angela was in just as much shock as he was.

Or that was how he preferred to see it.

He listened to the faint whipping of the long grass against the bodywork of the car as he took the corners ten or fifteen miles an hour too quickly, and then he carried on along the straighter stretch, what he supposed had once been a Roman road.

The car park was deserted. Well, it wasn't really a car park at all, but a mowed field. And when he pulled over the rugged terrain, feeling the car throw him all over the place, he noted that the fair-ground was no longer there—it had moved on.

Of course it had.

It had almost been two weeks since they'd come here last.

Still, he got out of the car and headed for the small cottage that stood on the other side of the field. Its chimney chugged away into the night sky, sending up cotton-wool smoke. He rapped on the door and asked after the fairground. The old lady there, who it turned out was the owner of the field, the leaser of the land, told him where the fairground had moved on to—gave him detailed directions.

As Randall got back behind the wheel, he surprised himself with his calmness. He wasn't shaking any more. That chill inside his chest had given him a certain detachment, made him think that all this was really just happening to someone else—someplace else.

He turned the heaters up to max and lost himself in the swell of dank, warm air that blew around the interior of his car, and then he barrelled through the darkened countryside once again.

12

THE GLOWING yellow-and-orange lights gave the fairground away. And Randall found himself concentrating so hard on the place, already scoping it out for the psychic's tent, that he almost missed the turning. He jammed the brakes and felt the car slide on the loose gravel pathway. He listened to the gravel pinging off the underside of the car. He stuck the car into its reverse gear, and with the *whine* of the engine thick in his ears, he sped backwards and took the turning into the field where the cars were parked.

He brought the car to a halt beside a people carrier—a dirty great van—and when he got out he managed to open the driver's door right into its side, leaving large dent. He stared at the damage for several seconds, lost in the gunmetal grey that showed through where he'd dinged the car.

Then he broke from his daze and set off into the fairground.

It all came back to him. One solid beam of detail. The hot, buttered popcorn popping. The candyfloss machine whirring away. The toffee-apple dip churning. He caught several glares from the vendors, and from parents too. He guessed he must look slightly manic, detached, a man without a family.

Which, he supposed, he was a third of the way to becoming.

He was a little surprised to feel his hair on end, so he smoothed it down a little. And he slowed his pace, wrapped his jacket around him as if it might ward off the fairground. All the sugar and butter in the air around here, it turned his stomach. He listened to children scream as a ride tossed them upside down. He saw their hair and clothing flap in the motion. And then, beyond the ride, he saw it. The mauve tent. The dwarf, in Edwardian costume, standing outside it, smoking away, his eyes slinking about the crowd—looking for another sucker.

Randall gritted his teeth. Only when he tasted blood in his mouth did he realise he was chewing his tongue too. He swallowed the blood all back and increased his pace, headed right for the tent.

When the dwarf spotted him, he dropped his cigarette on the ground and crushed it beneath his boot. He put on a smarmy grin. He still had that twinkle in his eye, and that attitude of his. "Back for more, eh?" he said, arching an eyebrow. He held out his palm. "Going rate hasn't changed, though. Tell you what, since I like your face I'll do you a discount. How's about we make it an even two pound, eh?"

Randall shoved past the dwarf, knocking him to one side.

"Hey! You can't go in there—she's busy!"

Randall bustled right through the flap to the tent and found himself inside. The joss sticks were burning. That acute odour stung his nostrils. But he didn't care. A girl of about twenty sat in the seat with her back to him. Mistress Margaret herself sat with her eyes shut, hands spread out over the crystal ball, doing that humming thing again.

The girl glanced back over her shoulder. She had on pink mascara and wore a tattered tracksuit top. Her face cratered like a volcano when she saw him there. "Get out, *you!* Wait your turn!"

Randall turned his attention to Mistress Margaret who, in the commotion, had opened her eyes and was now looking through the incense smoke at him. She parted her lips, stared him out a moment longer, then turned to her current client. When she spoke it was with that same soft voice he remembered from last time. "Albert would be glad to return your money, my dear, and I shall see you after. This," she said, giving Randall a pointed gaze, "is really quite important."

The girl pouted a moment, looked to Randall, then back to

Mistress Margaret, obviously weighing up her options. Then she got up from her seat and pushed past Randall, disappearing with a *flutter* of tent flap. And then Randal and Mistress Margaret were alone. She gestured for him to sit, but he had no intention of doing so.

None whatsoever.

Mistress Margaret smiled lightly.

Randall clenched his fists down by his sides, sure that he could punch her.

"You're still alive," she said, in a dry tone of voice.

"Night's not over yet."

Her smile widened. "Oh, you've passed the thirteen days. I think you'll find that destiny arrived right on time in this case."

"My wife's . . . she's . . ." He got another knot in his throat, but forced himself to finish what he had to say. "She's *dead*."

"Why, what did you think would happen, dear? You decided to make a deal with fate, you decided to change your destiny. Did you really think that it would be as simple as cheating death—that someone wouldn't have to pay?"

His eyes blazed and he surged forward. He leaped at Mistress Margaret and landed flat on the table, several inches short. There was a brief wobble and then the table collapsed beneath him with a series of splintering cracks. Randall lay there, rubbing his head, looking to Mistress Margaret who remained in her seat, apparently unmoved by this gesture.

The dwarf peered in through the tent flap. He looked to Randall and then whistled a shrill whistle. He looked to Mistress Margaret. "You, um, want us to take care of this one?"

"He was just leaving," she said, her voice now stern.

Randall's back and legs ached from the impact. His head, too, felt like it was on fire. He stumbled as he got back to his feet. He bore down on Mistress Margaret.

"You sure you're okay?" the dwarf said.

"Yes," Mistress Margaret replied. "Quite sure."

The dwarf glowered at Randall and then went back outside.

Mistress Margaret inspected her fingernails briefly and then fixed Randall with a steady glare. "What have you come here to get from me? I only tell the future—what you choose to do with it is none of my concern."

Again he felt anger smoulder through him. But he couldn't do anything.

He knew that it wouldn't change anything.

Her voice got sterner still. "Look, we can chat all you want about this, but it's going to cost you the going rate, I'm afraid. This is my profession, you see. However . . ." she paused, her stare finally falling on the skull which sat on the table beside her, ". . . it might be in your favour—in your *children's* favour—to let this lie." She locked eyes with him once more. "Hmm?"

Randall breathed in and out, feeling his lungs expand and contract. He had never felt anger like this—it was like a *madness*. And yet there was a voice, at the back of his mind, that told him that she was right. He had to leave this alone—just forget about it.

He had to pick up the pieces of his life.

Mourn his wife.

With a final exhale, like a defeated bull, he turned around and burst back out through the tent flap. He heard the dwarf shout after him.

"What does this look like, a freekin' charity? Hey! You! Don't you come back here!"

Randall got back in the car. All those fairground smells clung to his clothes again.

The candyfloss, the popcorn, the toffee apple.

He might never get clean again. This stench of the fairground might follow him around forever.

No, he was *sure* it would.

He slipped the keys into the ignition, gave the fairground one last glare, and then sped off into the night, never looking back in the rear-view mirror.

And never to return.

CORRIDOR OF HOPE

THE CORRIDOR stretches for miles and miles, this way and that, through darkness, through light, where it ends, no one knows. A light breeze blows through the hallways, always from East to West. It smells of something approximating the ocean: a slightly salty, stale—tired—odour.

An elderly gentleman limps along the dark-violet carpet, the hem of his charcoal cloak shimmering with each step. His name is Backrum. A set of keys jangles at his waist. He hums tunelessly under his breath, his lips hidden beneath the hood of the cloak.

He peruses the doors, absorbing the strange runes marking each as unique. He slows then draws to a stop, his breath coming hard and heavy as if creaking its way through his worn-out respiratory canals. With a shaky hand, he jabs the key into its lock and turns. He takes a deep breath and steps through.

His heart is like a windup clock, slowing to a stop, each motion of its mechanism lagging and awkward. He draws the door closed behind him and absorbs the room spread out ahead.

A white-washed bed stands before him. Pink flowers, with yellow filaments, are painted onto the base of the bed. A child sleeps soundly with the covers drawn up to her chest. In the gloom her flaming hair is rendered dim and colourless. Her cheeks, so rosy and freckle-born in the sunlight, are set in greyscale.

Backrum rests back on his heels, as if afraid to go any further, but he knows his task, knows that there's no other way. He takes an arthritic step forward and another until, gradually, he looms over the young girl's bed.

The girl murmurs in her sleep, some indistinguishable word. Her tiny fingers grip the hem of the bed sheet, squeezing then releasing in little five-second cycles.

From within his cloak, Backrum produces a vial of green liquid. It glows in the darkness, not of this world, or any other for that matter. He twists the cork and it pops lightly out of the vial. The liquid emits a light *hiss* and a coil of smoke twirls up into the air, as if doing battle with the very essence of this world.

A breath squeaks through Backrum's throat. He parts his lips slightly and tilts his head back as he holds the vial over the young girl, ready to pour. Just as the first drop of liquid nears the end of the vial, the young girl bats her eyelids, eyelashes like fly wings. Backrum hesitates, just for a moment, but, by the time he has composed himself it's too late. The girl is awake.

He keeps the vial still, in mid-air, unable to bring himself to move forward, to finish his task. It quivers in his fingertips and, for one precarious moment, it seems like the vial's going to drop to the floor and smash into a thousand pieces. But he strengthens his grip and stills himself.

The girl rubs her eyeballs with clenched fists, then she sits up in bed and scowls at him. She looks to be six or seven years old. "What you doing in my bedroom?"

Backrum sees the door, the portal back to the corridor, knows that he must retreat, leave this world behind, tail between his legs like some scolded mongrel. But he's rooted. It's impossible for him to leave this all behind now. He has been seen.

"Well?" she says, cocking her head to one side. "What you doing? I can get my mummy and daddy in here, you know."

Backrum corks the vial and returns it to the inner pocket of his cloak, wondering what to do next. They should be coming for him. His time must be up. He's been getting so slow recently, this seems as if it's the only result—just what he should've expected. Why should he return to the corridor? Why should he just hand himself in without a fight? No, he'll wait here, in this room, force them to carrying him away, fingernails dragging against floorboards, lungs bellowing.

The little girl peers into his eyes. "Are you my granddad?"

Backrum takes another shaky breath, then steadies himself on the bedpost. "Yes," he says. "In a way."

She straightens her back against the headboard and breaks into a grin. "I knew you would come, eventually."

"What . . . what did your parents tell you?"

"About my granddad?" she says, with a scowl. "They said that he lives in the woods, in a cabin, and he goes fishing for his dinner, every day." She looks him over. "Did you bring us any fish?"

Backrum glances to the portal, ready for them to come, but still they hold off. He turns his attention back to the girl. "Yes, I brought lots of fish. They're . . . they're downstairs, in the freezer."

She pokes her tongue out and wrinkles her nose. "Don't like fish."

"Why ever not?"

"Dunno, tastes fishy."

Through all the anxiety, the unknowing of when his end will come, Backrum conjures a smile, manages to look on the little girl as more than a mere morsel of the stretches and stretches, the plains and plains, of reality. In a way he's glad he didn't feed her the liquid, although he has no idea why. She will die, just like the rest—tethered to her mortal coil—just as he shall die too now that he's failed at his task.

She blinks up at him. "Whasa matter, Granddad? Are you tired?"

"Yes, a little."

"Sit down, then."

Seeing no chairs in the room, Backrum, still keeping the portal in his sights, perches down on the edge of the mattress. He inter-locks his fingers and closes his eyes. Blood drips and drabs through his temples, each pulse sending a pounding gale through his mind. He's suffered long and hard, and now they shall take him.

The girl reaches out and touches his hand, her nimble fingertips skirting the leathery wrinkles in his skin. "Wanna drink of water?"

He almost chuckles at the question, knowing that it would do him no good. He shakes his head. "No, thank you."

"You sad, Granddad?"

"A little."

"Why?"

He thinks about how he might go about explaining his situation, that in a matter of seconds, right now even, a group of otherworldly beings will burst through the portal and claim him, throw him right off this plain of reality—damn him forever.

"You crying?" she says, moving closer.

Her tiny body is like a radiator, flushing heat through him. It's been a long time since he's been close enough to a human to feel body heat. He wipes his eyes clean. "We all have to cry sometimes."

"Is it because Grandma's in heaven?"

Again, he has the urge to enlighten her, to tell her that things really aren't that simple. Wherever this girl believes her grandma to be, it's not some indistinct point above the atmosphere of Earth. "No," he says. "It's because I feel old."

The little girl gives him a side-on glance, studies his profile. "You're not really my granddad, are you?"

"No, I'm not."

She doesn't ask a follow-up question or make any effort to move away from him. When she speaks again, her voice is a whisper, almost husky in its conspiracy. "Who are you?"

He glances over to the portal, sure that they will take advantage of the pause in the conversation, dive out from wherever they lurk and seize him. But all that passes in the room is the gradual ticking of a clock with a cat's face which hangs on the opposite wall.

"Are you friends with my granddad?" she says.

When he breathes again he feels a sharp pain just below his ribcage. He looks down expecting to see a pitchfork jabbing him in the stomach but, instead, the little girl is poking him with her finger. A knot sticks in his throat and he swallows it back. "No, I'm not friends with your granddad."

Her eyes round in their sockets, curious and impressionable.

"I am the spirit of Chaos and Disorder."

"What's that mean?"

"It means that I slink my way round the recesses of several parallel worlds choosing tragedies, bringing misery into the lives of their beings, giving everyone a sense of perspective." He pauses briefly to consider his lexicon. "I make bad things happen."

The little girl averts her gaze, looks down at her fingers and scratches at dry skin in the centre of her palm. "Why'd you do that?"

He shrugs. "Because that's what I'm told to do."

"Do you like it?"

"No, not really."

She looks across the room, where a doll lies face down on the carpet, her stringy, woollen hair tousled. As she turns her head back toward him, a purple-silver flash passes over the portal. Then, barely noticeably, a pair of eyes dot the darkness—their irises a ruby red.

Backrum's time has come.

They make no attempt to come at him.

He never imagined it would be like this, that they wouldn't tear him out from his place. Deep down he knows this isn't his reality, he doesn't fit here. He should meet his destiny and be done with it.

Backrum rises from the bed.

"Where you going?" the little girl says.

The eyes smoulder in the gloom, sending waves of anger

through the air, toward him, the chastisement which will follow him forever.

He paces over the bedroom floor, ready to meet them head on.

"Wait!" the little girl says.

Backrum cranes his neck, looks back over his shoulder.

She steps out of bed and heads toward him. "Where you going?"

"I have to go now," Backrum says.

"Why?"

"Because it's my time."

"Are you going to heaven?"

"No, no I'm not."

The girl stands still, her shoulders rising and falling gently with her breathing.

"Goodbye," Backrum says, then steps into the portal.

As one world breaks apart, colours blending one into the other, moving in retrograde, he glances over at his companion.

It's a mondielk, thick brown fur covering its body and thick, muscular lips jutting out, proud, over its chin. It stands on its hind legs seemingly in defiance of the rules of whatever world it passes through.

"The girl?" Backrum says. "No one will hurt the girl?"

A shiver runs across the mondielk's fur.

"You won't send anyone else?" Backrum says.

The mondielk keeps its gaze fixed forward, looking ahead, through several plains of reality, into and out of various worlds, he doesn't speak again until they arrive back in the corridor, standing outside the door leading to the little girl's bedroom. "No," it says. "She shall not be harmed."

AUTHOR'S NOTE

Thank you for taking the time to read one of my books. If you would like to hear about my latest releases you can sign up for my newsletter here: www.raymondsflex.com

Thanks for reading!

Raymond S Flex

Worlds On Fire
A Short Story Collection